Slam
Dunk

KINGFISHER
Kingfisher Publications plc
New Penderel House
283-288 High Holborn
London WC1V 7HZ
www.kingfisherpub.com

First published in 2007
2 4 6 8 10 9 7 5 3 1

ISBN: 978 07534 1431 6

Printed in India
1TR/0707/THOM/SCHOY/80STO/C

Slam Dunk

DONNA KING

KINGFISHER

CHAPTER 1

Ashlee ran, weaved and jumped. She flipped the ball into the hoop from the 3-point line.

Tribeca Saints 31, SoHo Panthers 28 in the NYC Community League.

"Go, Saints! Go, Saints!" the fans yelled.

Five minutes to go to the end of the game and the Saints were edging ahead. But the Panthers had the ball; they were dribbling up the court – Ashlee fell back to defend.

"Yeah, Ashlee!" the Saints fans cried as she stole the ball back. She dribbled smoothly past half-court, faked in one direction to give herself an open space to drive to the basket, then pivoted and passed as a Panthers defender closed in. Marissa caught the ball, faked and passed back to Ashlee. This time Ashlee squared up to the hoop, tucked her elbows in and shot.

The ball kissed off the backboard and dropped through the net.

The referee signalled for two points – 33 to 28. The crowd went wild.

But Ashlee didn't notice them. She saw only the ball and her fellow teammates dressed in their brilliant blue uniforms – tall, lithe girls with long legs and arms that propelled them up to reach the hoop and tip the ball in. She heard only the voice of their coach, Erika Schrader, yelling instructions from the bench.

"Press!" Erika cried as the Panthers inbounded the ball.

The ref quickly blew her whistle, signalling that Marissa had fouled the Panthers' guard. Ashlee sprinted down the court and lined up for the foul shot. The

Panthers' guard shot the free throw off the front end of the rim, and Ashlee leapt up to grab the rebound. The Saints pushed the ball up the floor.

"Great defending!" the crowd roared.

For close on forty minutes they'd watched Ashlee Carson scoop, push, shoot and block the basketball. They'd seen her dribble circles round the Panthers team, twist her torso in mid-air and float the ball through that magical hoop.

Overhead, the rows of lights had dazzled. Out on the court the SoHo Panthers had been left floundering, flat-footed and frustrated.

"How does Ashlee do that?" the crowd cried in astonishment. "Honest to God, I swear I saw that girl fly!"

"Ashlee, where were you?" Theresa Carson was waiting grim-faced for her daughter at the door of their apartment. "I expected you home early tonight."

"The Saints had a game," Ashlee muttered. She flung her schoolbag down in the hallway and headed for the refrigerator.

"How come you never told me?"

"I did."

"I don't remember." Frowning, Theresa searched on the narrow hall table for her keys. "Listen, I'm late for work. I'm going to trust you to do your homework, then get to bed early. You look beat."

"'Hey, Ashlee, how did the game go? Did you win?'" Ashlee mimicked the voice of a sweet, supportive mom, the kind that wore lipstick and baked apple pie. The kind that didn't exist.

Theresa raised her eyebrows. She found her keys. "If I'm late again, I lose my job. If I lose my job, I don't buy your uniform for Queensbridge."

Ashlee frowned and shook her head. She said nothing.

"Do your homework," her mom

repeated, banging the door behind her as she left.

"Footwork fundamentals." Erika began Saturday's coaching session with the basics. She was focused on the four new kids who had joined the Tribeca Saints. "You stand with your weight forward on the balls of your feet, knees bent, hands at five and ten o'clock, butt down. Marissa, you show them."

Ashlee's best friend went into the familiar crouch while Ashlee sat tapping her foot on the sideline. In her head she ran through the new offensive formation that she wanted to practise with the rest of the team.

"From there you can slide left or right or shuffle backwards and forwards," Erika went on. "Simple," she grinned as Marissa demonstrated.

"Hey, Ashlee, where were you after the game last night?" Angelica leaned across the row of leggy girls, all dressed in jogging bottoms and Saints practice jerseys.

"Yeah, Ash, how come you didn't stay behind and celebrate?" Candice asked. "This is the first year ever that we beat the Panthers, and it was mostly down to you."

Ashlee shrugged. "Yeah, sorry. I couldn't make it." She didn't admit that she was at home doing her maths homework, or that her mom was on her case 110 percent of the time.

Ashlee, do your homework. Let me look at your science grade. See how hard I have to work waiting tables at La Sila to buy your uniform. Don't let me down, Ashlee. Work, work, work.

The Queensbridge scholarship exam was in two weeks' time. It loomed ever larger on her mother's horizon – the high peak of the Rocky Mountain range that was their life.

Up and down, up and down went the

Carson family fortunes. Ashlee remembered their life before her dad dumped her mom for a younger, prettier model. She was six years old at the time, the kind of blonde-haired, blue-eyed kid who had it all. There were sunny poolside pictures to prove it.

After her dad vanished for good, Ashlee and her mom had downsized big time. Gone was the luxurious waterside house in Miami. Hello to three rooms in a run-down brownstone in Tribeca – back to Theresa's roots in the old meatpacking district of New York. Rubbish and dirty snowdrifts lining the winter streets, the dash and rattle of the subway trains at the end of their street, the melting-pot school overlooking the wide Hudson where Ashlee first picked up a basketball and discovered she had a real talent.

"Ashlee?" Erika called. "Hey, wake up, girl. Didn't you hear me call the 'A' squad onto the court?"

Starting up from the bench, Ashlee

joined Marissa, Candice, Lindsay and Angelica. Here was action at last, to take her out of herself, to help her forget.

Erika studied Ashlee through narrowed eyes. "That's not like you," she snapped.

"Sorry. What are we doing here?"

"Showing the new kids how to fake," Marissa muttered from the corner of her mouth, handing Ashlee a ball.

"Begin with a head fake," Erika instructed. "Go!"

The five starters gathered at centre court and formed a large circle. They began passing the ball around, faking one way and pressing another.

"That's how you fake a defender – they think you're going to pass to the right, but you pass the opposite way. Lo and behold, you open up some space for a clean pass. Does that make sense?"

The four new kids nodded enthusiastically. They looked up at the starters with admiring glances as they swapped places with them on the floor.

"Ashlee, I want to talk," Erika said, leaving Marissa, Lindsay, Candice and Angelica in charge of coaching the four new recruits. The coach took Ashlee off to the side.

"Are you OK?" she checked.

Ashlee nodded. "Sorry about earlier," she said, blushing. "I had my mind on other things."

"Anything I can help with?"

"No, it's cool."

"Come on, I may look as if I bite, but I promise I won't," Erika urged. She'd been coaching for fifteen years – drilling, teaching them the drop step, the jump shot, the 'give and go'. She prided herself on being able to read a kid's personality as well as anyone.

"No, really." When it came to personal stuff, Ashlee always did this. She shut up tight as a clam. Or she said everything was cool. She faked it off the court as well as on.

Erika sat Ashlee down on the bench. "OK, so let's take a long, cool look at things. First, I want to tell you how happy I was with your performance last night at point. I was impressed with your leadership qualities – your ability to read the game and motivate the other players. I'd like you to keep that position for the rest of the season."

"Wow!" Ashlee took a deep breath as her roller-coaster life took a sudden upturn. *Hold on tight!*

"Yeah, wow! But seriously, Ashlee, I have high hopes for you."

"Thanks, Erika. I love playing point guard and I won't let you down."

The coach's steel-grey eyes looked deep into Ashlee's blue ones. "You're good enough to make it to the top in women's basketball," she confided. "I mean it, kid, you're heading for the heights – for the junior regional teams and then the nationals, if you want it enough."

Ashlee gave her head a quick shake as she tried to take it all in, then nodded. "I want it!"

"Enough?" Erika double-checked.

"I love playing basketball!" Ashlee insisted. "I live it, breathe it, sleep it. It's all I ever want to do!"

"And nothing's going to stop you?" Erika asked.

At that moment Ashlee felt like one of the subway trains rattling headlong down the track, hurtling through the stations to its final destination. "Nothing," she promised. "When I'm out there on that court, I want to win, believe me!"

CHAPTER 2

Ashlee sprawled on the couch, her attention superglued to the TV screen.

She watched her hero, Michael Jordan, split from two defenders, then take off from just inside the key for a majestic one-handed dunk.

Rewind. Play that again. See how King Michael focuses on that hoop, how the ball was never going anywhere except into the net.

Listen to "His Airness" talk about his basketball ambitions as a kid – how being cut from his sophomore high-school team only fuelled his drive to get better – and ultimately landed him at the University of North Carolina, where he helped win an

NCAA Championship. From there, he went on to the Olympics and got a gold medal. He followed that with an unbelievable career with the Chicago Bulls and the Washington Wizards.

I could do that, Ashlee thought. *I could defy gravity and make amazing leaps. I could be an Olympic gold medallist and a WNBA All-Star!*

Once, long ago, in her previous life, she'd met her idol face to face.

At four years old she'd been hoisted onto her dad's shoulders and taken behind the scenes at a Wizards game to shake hands with Michael Jordan. It had been his final season as a player. He was already and forever a basketball god.

She still remembered the razzmatazz of the cheerleaders with their pompoms, Michael's warm smile and the roar of the crowd in the background . . .

"OK, that's the end of downtime for today." Theresa marched in front of the TV and switched it off. "You spend way too much time watching that old DVD instead of concentrating on your schoolwork."

"Mom, it's Sunday. Give me a break."

"Sunday is the best day to make progress with your studies," Theresa insisted. "No distractions. No excuses."

Every weekend it was the same – the moment Theresa found Ashlee chilling on the couch, she waded in with the schoolwork stuff. "When do I get to hang?" Ashlee demanded, deliberately slouching further into the soft cushions.

Her mom shrugged. "When do I?" she retorted. She worked at the pizza and pasta restaurant six days a week. The rest of the time she shopped for groceries and cleaned the house, keeping things going as best she could.

Ashlee sighed and sprang up from the couch. "You're weird, Mom. You know that?"

"Yeah, *weird*. Weird to want you to get this scholarship. Weird to want my daughter to do well in her studies and become a doctor instead of a waitress like her mother."

"OK, point taken. But it's become a big thing with you – like an obsession." Ashlee was in the mood for a fight.

"Don't use that tone," Theresa warned. "Think about it, Ash. The reason you have no time to hang out is not your schoolwork but the Saints. That team takes up every minute of your free time."

"Oh jeez, not this again!" Ashlee groaned. She headed for her room but her mom followed her.

"You know I'm OK with the sport in school," Theresa went on. "It's good to keep fit – no problem. But I don't like it spilling out into your spare time with the Saints. That's what I object to."

"Object away," Ashlee retorted. She sat in front of her mirror and fixed her long blonde hair into a high ponytail. "It doesn't matter – I still plan to play with the Saints. Erika made me the starting point guard for the season, if only you bothered to ask!"

For a moment Theresa fell silent, staring at her daughter's reflection in the mirror. Something from way back in the past reared up and scared her. Maybe the fact that at five feet ten inches tall and with those wide blue eyes and blonde hair, Ashlee reminded Theresa now and every waking moment of her father, Robert. She took a sharp intake of breath.

"Why are you staring?" Ashlee demanded, slamming down her hairbrush.

"No reason." Theresa crushed down the storm of feelings that threatened to engulf her. She spoke coldly. "Here's the way it is, Ashlee. Either you voluntarily make more time for your schoolwork in the final run-up to the scholarship exam or I get tough and make you give up the Saints for the season."

Ashlee gasped and swung round. "You

can't force me to do that!"

Theresa pressed her lips together, looking determined. "I can and I will," she said coldly. "So no more arguing. School comes first, Ashlee, whether you like it or not."

"OK, so how come you didn't apply for the USA Women's Youth Basketball Camp yet?" Marissa wanted to know.

Ashlee skipped sideways to avoid a sludgy, half-frozen puddle and bumped into an old woman walking a dog. "Because!" she replied.

"Because what?" Turning the corner onto windy Hudson Street, Marissa pulled her woollen hat further down over her forehead. "Listen, if you don't make the Miami Development Camp, you have no chance of reaching the Junior National Trials in Puerto Rico this summer."

"Don't tell me," Ashlee muttered. She and Marissa were heading over to meet Angelica at the corner of Duane Park, from where they would walk to the gym. "Tell my mother!"

Marissa clicked her tongue against her teeth. "Oh yeah, I forgot."

"How could you forget the dragon lady that is my mom?" Ashlee said with a laugh. "You know – the one that stands guard at the door of my apartment and breathes fire at my friends whenever they come over."

"She won't let you apply, huh?"

"Worse," Ashlee confessed. "Her latest move is to threaten to pull me out of the Saints if I don't work harder for the scholarship."

"Work *harder*?" Marissa knew that Ashlee already studied 24-7. Waving to attract Angelica's attention at the park gate, she shook her head in disbelief. "What does she want—a pointy-headed freak for a daughter?"

"Actually, yeah," Ashlee sighed and paused. "One thing's for sure, she doesn't want me to be a basketball player."

"Like your dad," Marissa realized.

Like Robert Elkin, who played for Miami Heat in the early 1990s and burned out spectacularly on booze and women.

Ashlee nodded. "You got it," she said quietly, before Angelica ran up to join them and the subject switched to a drop-dead-gorgeous guy Angelica had just seen heading into the recreation centre through the revolving door.

Ashlee stayed late at the centre long after Marissa and Angelica had gone off on the trail of the mythical cute guy. She had plenty of time to put in some shooting practice and still arrive home before her mom got back from work.

She wanted to improve the backspin on her release, which meant a stronger flip of her wrist. She started close to the basket, aiming and shooting, then taking two steps backwards each time until she reached the three-point line. It was a routine she repeated ten times with total concentration before she decided to stop and take a shower.

As the hot water tingled on her skin, encasing her in steam inside the cubicle, Ashlee thought again about what Marissa had said. And yeah, for sure her dad was at the root of her mom's problem with basketball. Theresa could obsess about the Queensbridge scholarship and Ashlee's future all she liked, but really it was what had happened way back in the past with her dad.

"Huh!" Ashlee tilted her face to meet the full force of the shower. Sometimes it took an outsider to make you see things the way they were. And Marissa was a good friend – one of the best.

"I get it!" Ashlee said out loud. "For the first time in my life, I really get where Mom's coming from!"

★★★

"Mom, we need to talk," Ashlee began.

It was late on Sunday night. She's been sitting at the desk in her room when her mom got home, but Theresa had smelled shampoo and spotted Ashlee's wet hair. She'd guessed Ashlee had been down at the gym again.

"What's there to talk about?" Theresa said wearily. "I go to work, leaving you to study. You disobey me and hang out with your friends instead. End of story."

Ashlee bit her tongue. She wasn't going to enter into an argument about the fact that she'd finished her schoolwork before she went out. This was something much more important. "It's about Dad," she insisted.

Theresa sank onto the couch and closed her eyes. "Did he call?"

Ashlee's heart was in her mouth as she said what was on her mind. "No. I haven't talked with him since Christmas. What I'm saying is, Dad is the real reason you don't want me to play basketball, isn't it?"

Her mom suddenly opened her eyes. They were startled and defensive.

"It's not the scholarship," Ashlee went on. "Face it, Mom. You and I both know I can breeze through these tests, no problem. And that's not me shooting off my big mouth – it's what the teachers told you at parents' evening, it's what they say in front of me every day to the other kids: 'You work as hard as Ashlee Carson, blah, blah, blah, and you'll be a straight-A student too!'"

"You still need to work," her mom said bleakly. "You can't afford to slacken off now."

"Mom, are you listening to me? I can do it. I can stroll into Queensbridge and you know it. But it's Dad and what he did to us that makes stuff complicated around here."

"That's not true, Ashlee. You're just a kid. You don't know what you're saying."

Ashlee shook her head. "You won't admit it, but that's why you don't support me, why you won't come to watch my games, why you switch off every time I talk about basketball."

"Enough with the accusations," Theresa sighed. She got up and went through to the tiny kitchen, where she made strong black coffee for herself and poured orange juice for Ashlee without asking. "I only think about what's best for you, even though you seem to find that hard to believe."

Ashlee stared at her mom's back – at the long, dark hair twisted and pinned high on her head, at the white shirt and neat black skirt that she wore to wait tables. "Forget it. And forget the OJ," she snapped, storming off to her room.

That was what happened in her family when she tried to open up on dark, deep stuff – a back was turned and she got treated like a little kid.

★★★

Ashlee flopped down on her bed. OK then, no way would she try to talk to her mom ever again. Instead, she would go ahead and ask Erika to get her a place at the Youth Festival. She would do it tomorrow and she wouldn't tell Theresa, because no way was the stupid scholarship going to come between Ashlee and basketball success.

"How much do you want it?" the coach had asked her.

"Enough!" she had replied.

Enough to disobey and to keep secrets. Enough to lie and pretend.

Nothing was going to stop this subway train. One day soon she was going to be the Most Valuable Player in the WNBA. She would set her mind to it. Then she, Ashlee Carson, would be like His Airness. She would lead her team to a championship – and then on to stardom!

CHAPTER 3

Brooklyn All-Stars 16, Tribeca Saints 12.

The Saints had called for time-out midway through the first half. Erika gathered her team on the bench.

"Lindsay, that's your third technical foul in five minutes," Erika warned the tall centre. "I want you to cool down for a while. Courtney, you're in. Candice, your game isn't up to scratch today either. You can sit on the bench with Lindsay. Tiffany, this is your chance to shine."

As the coach made the substitutions, Ashlee tried to figure out where the team was going wrong.

OK, so the All Stars were strong in defence, plus the ref was calling a tight game, but that wasn't why they were losing. *It's down to me,* Ashlee decided. *I'm not reading Marissa's cuts to the basket and I'm not passing to Angelica when she's open. Face it, I'm not focused!*

Timeout ticked away as Ashlee pinpointed the problem for herself. When the official signalled for the clock to restart, she was on her toes and ready to go.

"Good block, Ashlee!" the supporters cheered, urging their team forward. "Hey, neat dribble, Courtney! Go, Saints, go!'

Ashlee collected the ball from Courtney's inbound pass then dribbled up the court. She threw up both arms in protest as her defender leaned in and swiped at the ball, thrusting Ashlee off balance.

But the ref ignored the foul and allowed the All Stars centre to steal the ball and speed towards their hoop. Ashlee was on her tail and closed her out with quick, choppy steps, forcing her to make a rushed shot that rolled out of the hoop. Ashlee rebounded the ball.

"Go, Ashlee!" the supporters chanted.

In the coach's box, Erika was up on her feet, willing Ashlee to score.

Ashlee pushed the ball back up the court and passed to Courtney. Courtney faked right and hit Ashlee with a chest-pass as she cut towards the hoop. She was open – no teammates nearby – and two All-Stars moving towards her. It had to be a long, accurate shot. She leaned back, took aim and, with a strong flick of her wrist, she shot.

The ball soared through the air to sudden silence and intake of breath. It flew straight and true, dropping clean through the hoop.

Erika punched the air as the gap between the teams narrowed to one point. The crowd went wild.

"Let's go!" Ashlee muttered to her team-mates. The pressure was on; they had to keep up the momentum.

Marissa grinned. "Now we're cooking!"

The Saints surged through the rest of the half, scoring four more baskets while the All-Stars defence fell apart. At the half-time break the score stood at 26 points to 16.

"Hard work and hustle!" Erika told her team, gathering them round in a close huddle. "That's the secret for the rest of this game. Whatever you do from now on in, keep possession of the ball. Ashlee, keep up your intensity – don't slack off, OK?"

Taking deep breaths, Ashlee nodded. She knew she was back on form and that it was all to do with attitude. *Hustle*! she repeated to herself.

"And Marissa, no need to be flashy out there," Erika warned. "Just be a team player, see what's going on across the whole floor, like Ashlee."

With the coach's advice running fresh

in their veins, the Saints took to the floor for the second half. The All-Stars seemed revived by the team talk too. They started with the ball and raced towards the Saints' hoop.

"Angelica, switch!" Ashlee yelled as the tallest All-Stars player faked and cut past Courtney.

The All-Stars forward dodged Angelica then shot from just outside the key, but Ashlee was already there. She leaped high in the air, twisting her body so that her right arm could swat the ball away.

Down the court, bouncing the ball, dancing to an unheard rhythm. Foot-fake to the left, drive through to the right, make the lay-up.

Two more points. On a roll, heading for victory.

Final score – Tribeca Saints 46, Brooklyn All-Stars 29.

"So, I hear you and Marissa both made

successful applications to the Youth Basketball Camp next week." Erika spoke to Ashlee with evident pride.

It was straight after the All–Stars game, late in the evening as the gym emptied and the attendants switched off the lights.

Ashlee zipped up her jacket and walked out into the dark street with her coach. Electronic ads for lipgloss and limos, new movies and long–lash mascara flashed on giant billboards. "Yeah, I'm pretty excited about it," she confessed. "Thanks for putting my application through at the last minute."

"There's a big roster this year," Erika warned her. "You need to play your best game to shine in the crowd."

"I will." *I will! I will!*

The coach stopped under a street lamp, hands in pockets, looking her protégée straight in the eye. "Ashlee, do you know what sets an exceptional player apart from a merely talented one?"

Quickly, Ashlee shook her head.

"It's making the big play at crunch time like you did tonight. It's taking it to the hoop through drive and sheer willpower. Do you understand what I'm saying?"

"I think so," Ashlee nodded.

"Don't just think – *know*! That nugget of knowledge is power."

Once more Ashlee nodded, this time meeting Erika's eyes with more confidence.

Slowly the coach's intense gaze softened and she changed the subject. "Will your folks get to Miami for the camp?" she asked.

Ashlee blushed. "No. My mom doesn't like to watch me play."

"Ah yes, I forgot. And how about your dad? Is he a fan?"

"Yeah, he likes the game." Confusion at the mention of her dad set Ashlee's cheeks aflame. "Actually, he used to play professionally."

Erika's eyes widened. She'd coached

Ashlee Carson for six whole years and this was news to her. 'So that's where you get your talent! How come I never knew that?'

"Because I don't talk about it. I hardly ever see my dad. He left when I was a little kid."

"Yeah, but a pro! Maybe I've heard of him. Who is he?"

Ashlee took a deep breath. She was in too deep to pull back. "His name's Robert Elkin," she confessed in a voice not much above a whisper.

"Robert Elkin of Miami Heat!" Erika gasped. "Girl, you're full of surprises. I'm telling you, Robert Elkin at the height of his game was magnificent."

"As good as Michael Jordan?" Ashlee asked with a dry, nervous laugh. What had made her break her silence over her dad right here, right now? Was she crazy?

Erika laughed out loud. "No one even touches the hem of Michael Jordan's baggie shorts! Not even your dad, Ashlee.

But Elkin was up there in the late eighties," she insisted. "Believe me, he was a *player*!"

"Ashlee, you didn't!" Marissa exclaimed. "Your mom will go crazy if she finds out!"

The two girls were talking outside science class, before the teacher arrived. Ashlee had just broken the news to Marissa that she'd made secret contact with her dad.

OK, so this really was a big deal – calling Robert from out of the blue, nursing an idea that might just get her to the camp without her mom blocking her way.

She'd come up with it as she was lying in bed the night before. She'd been mulling over what she'd told Erika and remembering the way her coach's eyes had lit up when she'd mentioned Robert Elkin. And it had come to Ashlee in a flash – one of those wild ideas that take hold and run away with you – that she could go behind her mom's back and get to Miami without telling her.

Sure, it would involve a few lies. But if she told Theresa the truth there would be the biggest fight and Ashlee would be bound to lose, the way her mom was acting recently over the scholarship.

Do I have the guts to do it? she'd asked herself in the dark room. Then, *How much do I want to get to this festival?* The answers had bounced like ping-pong balls inside her head, this way and that. In the end, she recalled what Erika had said about taking it to the hoop through drive and willpower. *That's what I need to do right now,* she'd decided. Then she'd taken out her phone and dialled the number.

"Your mom will go crazy!" Marissa insisted now.

"Mom won't know," Ashlee explained. "I called Dad from my cell phone and told him I needed a plane ticket to Miami. I made him promise not to blab."

There had been a long silence. Then her dad had said he would fix it for her. No questions. No arguments

"I'm going to the Youth Development Camp," Ashlee had told him. "My coach, Erika Schrader, set it up for me."

Another silence.

"She figures I can make it through the camp to the Junior Nationals in Puerto Rico. Listen, Dad – Mom doesn't have to know anything about this, OK?"

But just then the connection had broken up and her dad hadn't called back. All Ashlee could do was wait, and hope and pray that the plane tickets would arrive in the post.

Now Marissa was standing in the school corridor, open-mouthed. "Oh my God, what excuse will you use?"

"I'll say I'm staying over at your place." Ashlee had already worked out what she would tell her mom. "The camp is over the long weekend, right after my scholarship exam. I'll tell Mom I deserve a break and I'm going to chill at your house for the weekend."

Marissa thought for a while then nodded. "OK. But what if she checks out your story with my mom?"

Mr Baron, the science teacher, was walking down the corridor towards them. "She won't," Ashlee assured Marissa hurriedly. "Mom will be so stressed out with work and everything, and so relieved I finally took the Queensbridge entrance exam that she won't make that call. Marissa, will you back up my story or not?"

Her friend frowned as the science teacher ushered them both into the lab. "OK, Ash," she muttered. "But gee, I hope you know what you're doing!"

That weekend Ashlee kept her mom happy and put in the work for the scholarship. She needed to score well in science and maths, so on Saturday she ran through the main topics again and again, drilling herself and making sure the facts were stored in her head.

"This is the last big push," her mom reminded her, pleased to see her daughter sprawled on her bed, surrounded by sheets of revision papers.

"Yeah, I know. By the way, Marissa wants me to hang out at her house this weekend to chill out after the exam. I told her it was cool."

Theresa only half listened as she sorted through the morning post. Junk mail, more junk mail, a credit-card statement – a letter postmarked Miami for Ashlee . . .

Ashlee looked up and caught her mom's surprised expression. She saw the long white envelope and jumped up to snatch it from her. "It's from Dad," she muttered, sliding it unopened under her pillow.

Theresa frowned. "I see that. But since when does he write to you?"

Ashlee flashed her an angry look. "I *am* his daughter, remember?"

Her mom turned away. "Maybe *he* should remember that a little more often," she said under her breath. She almost turned back into Ashlee's room, then changed her mind.

Ashlee took a deep breath. Not until she was sure that her mom had collected her keys and left for work did she sneak another look at the precious letter. She took it out from under the pillow, turned it face up, felt the oblong cardboard shape of the plane ticket inside. For a long while she held it between trembling fingers and stared at the smooth white envelope.

She opened it at last. Inside there was a scrawled note from her dad. "Will meet you at airport. See you Friday. Robert." Plus the longed-for ticket – Ashlee's passport out of her mom's world of waiting tables, pressure and stress. An entry into the world she dreamed of.

★★★

Harlem Suns 26, Tribeca Saints 29. Six minutes to play and Suns called time-out. They regrouped and planned their final minutes of the game. The Suns subbed in a new player from the bench. She was fast and aggressive, stealing the ball from Courtney and then from Ashlee for an easy lay-up. The Harlem team now had a narrow lead.

Ashlee was cross with herself. How had she lost possession and conceded the lead? She'd failed to protect her dribble, and the subbed-in number 8 had quick hands and good footwork.

"Go, Suns!" The noisy supporters yelled and cheered with three minutes left on the clock.

"Watch out for the pick-and-roll!" Erika warned from the bench.

This time Ashlee read it right and slid by the approaching Harlem player, staying with the ball. These girls were good – tall and athletic, easily the best team the Saints had played all season.

As Ashlee intercepted the pass and raced towards the hoop, closely followed by the Suns' number 8, she set her mind on payback. In a flash she tossed the ball to Angelica, who raced ahead and was quickly approaching the three-point line.

Angelica faked a jump shot but passed the ball back to Ashlee instead. *Quick thinking!* Ashlee caught, dribbled once, and layed the ball up and into the basket.

Harlem Suns 30, Tribeca Saints 32. One minute to play.

Don't foul. Don't foul! Her coach's words echoed in Ashlee's mind. The Saints settled into their half-court defence as the Suns approached. The Suns' guard dribbled and passed the ball around the perimeter looking for their point of attack. A pass down low was deflected but soon recovered by the Harlem shooting guard, who brought the ball up top to regroup.

Then, suddenly, she broke towards the basket, determined to score.

Ashlee quickly switched into defensive mode and slid gracefully between the hoop and the explosive Harlem guard. The two collided, and the whistle blew.

"Offensive foul!" the ref yelled.

"Hustle!" Erika yelled from the bench. "Ashlee, slow the game down and spread the court out. Keep possession. Hang on in there!"

With only seconds left, the Saints inbounded the ball and moments later the final horn blared. The game was won!

Ashlee disappeared under a group of grinning, backslapping teammates, a bright blue knot of entangled arms and legs in the centre of the floor.

And it was the best feeling imaginable to emerge from the celebrating group — on top of the world, knowing that you could do anything, go anywhere and never be afraid of anything or anyone ever again!

"Good job!" Erika grinned at her. Her team had won the hardest game of the season. Her point guard had held the Saints together and led them to victory. "And good luck for Miami," she added. "You go, girl. Don't let anything stop you now!"

CHAPTER 4

"I still don't feel comfortable with this," Marissa confessed to Ashlee.

They sat on Ashlee's bed early on Monday evening, writing lists of the stuff they needed to take to Miami. The bedroom door was shut and Marissa spoke in a whisper.

Ashlee frowned. "Which bit exactly don't you like?"

"The bit about lying to your mom."

Two pairs of Air Jordan trainers, two pairs of jogging pants, four T-shirts, two sweatshirts . . . Ashlee went systematically down her list. "Is two sweatshirts enough?"

"Ash! Listen to what I'm saying – what

if your mom finds out?"

"She won't. Maybe I should cut back on the shirts and take three sweatshirts. Uh-oh, no, I forgot. It'll be hot in Florida, even at this time of year."

"We're in deep trouble if she finds out. How come you're doing the ostrich thing over this?"

At last Ashlee looked up. "Sticking my head in the sand?"

"Yeah, you're totally in denial. This is one huge risk you're taking."

"And you don't want to help me?" Ashlee said accusingly, feeling suddenly angry with Marissa. "You've only known me since we were seven years old. We've only been best buddies since we were nine!"

Marissa sighed and shook her head. "Don't worry, I won't drop you in it. But I'm worried, Ash. Worried for you."

Ashlee echoed Marissa's sigh. "What else can I do? If Mom knew I was spending part of this week training with

Erika instead of studying full time, she'd go crazy. On the other hand, if I don't put in the time with my coach, I have no chance of making a good impression at the camp. There's nothing else I can do."

"But what about your dad?" Marissa picked up on another point that Ashlee had been trying to forget. "How come he's Mr Generosity all of a sudden, sending you the plane tickets and everything?"

Ashlee shrugged. "I got the tickets — that's all that matters."

With eyes half closed and long legs crossed, Marissa gazed at the Michael Jordan posters on Ashlee's wall. "Yeah, well," she said, giving in. "Let's hope this works."

The girls jumped at the click of the door handle and quickly hid their lists as Theresa poked her head into the room.

"Yeah, yeah, I know, I'm out of here," Marissa said hastily. "Ashlee has to study and I'm stopping her. I'm gone already. Bye!"

Theresa came in as Marissa shot out past her. "Where's your programme for this evening?" she asked, turning over pieces of paper on Ashlee's desk.

"Inside my head."

"You should write it down. Then you can check off topics as you get through them."

"Mom, who's sitting this test?" Ashlee objected. She'd been careful to hide the plane tickets in an inside pocket of her schoolbag, but she still felt uneasy as her mom went through her stuff.

"What news from your dad?" Theresa asked, trying to sound casual but failing. "In the letter he sent you – what news?"

"The usual," Ashlee mumbled. "That is, no news. You know Dad."

"So why write?" Theresa persisted.

Ashlee shrugged.

"You're being very secretive. Can I see the letter?"

"No way, Mom – it was addressed to me. Anyway, I read it and threw it out."

Feeling hot and angry, Ashlee pushed her mom aside from her desk and sat down. "I need to work, OK?"

"I don't trust Robert," Theresa sighed, reluctant to drop the subject. "What does he want?"

"Nothing. Zilch. Zero." Head down, Ashlee shut her mother out.

Theresa stared at the back of Ashlee's head, again getting the dreaded feeling that her daughter was turning out too much like her father for comfort. But there was nothing she could do. At least now basketball was taking a back seat, and Ashlee seemed focused on the scholarship. Counting her blessings, Theresa backed down and closed the door.

"So what are your weak points?" Erika asked Ashlee.

It was after school on Tuesday and they were practising in the school gym. As usual, Ashlee had lied to Theresa. She had told her she planned to study in the library that evening.

Erika's question took Ashlee by surprise. She had to think this one through. "I guess I don't always see the whole court," she admitted. "I focus too much on my own space."

Erika, dressed in a blue tracksuit with a big white scarf wrapped high around her neck, nodded. "Always be aware of your teammates. To find the right pass takes split-second timing. So does taking it to the hoop. Awareness. It comes with experience."

As she listened to the veteran coach, Ashlee nodded. Though it was chilly inside the gym and they could see their breath in the cold air, she was relaxed and warm after fifteen minutes of lay-up drills. "And I guess my leg strength could be better," she admitted.

Again Erika nodded. "A little more running, and skipping ten minutes per day will put that right. How about mental toughness, Ashlee? This is still the big question. Do you think you have that?"

Ashlee stood with her hands on hips. She looked up at the high overhead lights, listening to Erika's voice echo around the empty hall. "What exactly does it mean – 'mental toughness'?" she queried. "Do I have to be a hard and selfish person to reach the top? Is that what you're saying?"

"No way!" Erika replied. "I'm talking the opposite. A selfish player gets nowhere. You have to be open and adaptable. I can see both those qualities in you – no problem."

"So how do you mean, 'tough'?" Ashlee was puzzled.

Erika tried to put it a way that Ashlee would understand. "Take your hero, Michael Jordan. He was a likeable guy. Real popular – right?"

Ashlee nodded. In a flash she pictured the grace of Michael in motion – easy, fluid, graceful, not openly aggressive.

"The man had dignity," Erika went on.

"And charisma. There were nine other players on the court but he was the only one you wanted to watch."

"Yeah," Ashlee agreed. She totally saw what Erika was saying.

"And yet, you know what?" the coach said with a smile. "Michael Jordan was also the most determined and tenacious player you ever saw. His willpower dominated the floor. He hated to lose."

"Yeah, I get it."

"No, listen. The people who knew him best – the other players – they were in awe. I remember one guy telling me the way he saw Michael. He told me that behind the Mr Nice Guy presentation, Michael had the athletic heart of an assassin."

A shiver went down Ashlee's spine. She instantly saw an image of Michael Jordan's face when he made the big play. Eyes focused; tongue out slightly as he cut through the air. "You're talking about the will to win?"

"Above all else," Erika insisted. "A lot of girls have that trained out of them by the time they get to high school. It's not feminine, it's not cool. Besides, it has to do with how you're wired in the first place."

"Wired to win!" Ashlee got it one hundred percent.

"It's either in your heart or it's not," the coach concluded. "If it's there, you'll be unbeatable."

"Well then, I hope I have it," Ashlee said with quiet determination.

Erika gave her one of those close, intense stares. "Time will tell," she murmured, walking to the door and switching off the lights.

"We're staying at the Miami Sheraton," Marissa said. "My dad has taken two days off work to be there. My mom's feeding me up on proteins and high carb stuff for energy."

"Who are you flying with?" Ashlee wanted to know. It was already Wednesday afternoon. The week was whizzing by.

"We're flying Delta. How about you?"

"American Airlines from JFK. I check in at 2 o'clock." Ashlee's exam ended at midday. She had two hours to get across town to the airport. Talk of Marissa's mum and dad and the flash hotel somehow unsettled her.

"The same as us," Marissa realised. "Hey, you can meet me and share our taxi!"

Ashlee shook her head. "No, it's easier for me to use the subway. I have it all worked out."

"You're sure?" Marissa checked. They were standing on a street corner talking over the blare of car horns and rumble of traffic. "You know something? My stomach is already tied in knots every time I think about getting on that plane. How about you? Are you nervous?"

"Yeah," Ashlee agreed. Her head was full of scholarship stuff – the anatomy of the human body for science, algebraic equations for maths. Facts were bursting out of her brain.

And on top of that she had the tension of getting out there on the basketball court and proving she could play well. Not just "play well", but be the best. Running, jumping shooting, scoring. Better than the other girls. Better even than Marissa. Unbeatable.

"We can do it," Marissa assured her. "You wait and see."

On Thursday Ashlee woke with a stomach ache.

"You look pale," her mom commented at breakfast. "Are you sick?"

Today she had school and then coaching with Erika. After that, two hours of final revision for the test. And last thing that evening, before her mom got back from the restaurant, Ashlee would secretly pack her bag for Miami. "I'm fine," she replied.

"Maybe take it easy tonight," Theresa

suggested. "Go to bed early and wake up fresh for the exam."

Ashlee stared back at her then cupped her hand round her ear. "I didn't quite get that. Could you run it by me again?"

"I said, *take it easy*." Her mom gave a faint smile. "And don't look at me like that!"

"Did you remember I'm staying over at Marissa's place this weekend?" Ashlee quickly took advantage of her mom's moment of weakness. "I'm going there straight from school."

Theresa looked up sharply. "But how will I know how you did in your exam?"

"I'll call you." Ashlee zipped up her jacket and picked up her schoolbag. "In any case, you won't be home tomorrow afternoon. You'll be at work."

"But I want to see you when I get back." Suddenly Theresa looked like she would back out of the weekend deal.

"I already fixed it up with Marissa!" Ashlee gabbled, heading for the door. "I can't let her down!"

Sleep wouldn't come to Ashlee that night. Her mind raced; her tired body fidgeted this way and that.

True, she'd fitted in everything she'd planned – her schoolwork followed by a session with Erika, followed by study for the test and then packing.

"Ashlee, where's your head today?" her English teacher had asked. 'Did you even hear the question I asked?'

Erika had given her one last piece of advice. "Stay cool and focused. Remember everything you learned."

Ashlee had got through it all but she couldn't rest. She looked back on her crowded, secretive day and forward to the check-in at JFK, side-stepping the crucial morning test that held all her mom's hopes and dreams.

What if I'm late and they won't let me on the plane? she asked herself. *What happens if*

I arrive in Miami and Dad isn't there? What do I do then?

She turned over in bed and pulled the covers over her head.

He's Mr Unreliable, remember! She heard the warning inner voice. *He's the guy who ditched Mom, and incidentally left you behind too — like lost baggage, or a heavy item that couldn't be taken along on the conveyor belt of his life.*

She tossed and turned again.

Say he comes to the airport and you meet him, how will he be? Will he even be sober?

"Don't think about it!" Ashlee muttered. She glanced at her bedside clock. It was a quarter past three. Turning onto her back, she stared up at the dark ceiling.

CHAPTER 5

Queensbridge School was impressive. It was one of those old buildings with fancy ceilings and mock pillars. The tall windows had tiny diamond-shaped panes of leaded glass.

Ashlee filed into the school early on Friday morning, along with fifty or so other scholarship hopefuls. She was the tallest by far.

Her mom had sent her off with tears and prayers. "I'm so proud of you," she'd whispered, clutching Ashlee's hand. "I never thought I'd see the day that my daughter would be sitting the exam for a school like Queensbridge. It's a doorway to a great future, God willing!"

"Hey Mom, slow down. I didn't even take the test yet." Ashlee's attention had been on getting her sports bag containing her kit and the plane tickets out of the apartment without a comment from her mom.

Theresa had wiped her wet cheeks with the back of her hand. "I know. And listen, if you don't get the scholarship, we'll deal with it somehow. I mean, the point is, you will have tried your best."

Ashlee grimaced now as she sat in the examination hall and remembered the parting conversation. Her mom didn't know it, but she had a trick of piling on the guilt. Sitting at a desk in a long row of students, Ashlee decided that for her mom's sake she had to give the test her best shot.

"Jeez, that was tough!" The girl at the desk behind Ashlee leaned forward after the exam was over and the papers had been handed in. "Did you know the answer to question 6b? Was it the metatarsal or the metacarpal?"

"Metatarsal," Ashlee answered. "I'm ninety percent sure on that." Throughout the test she'd felt calm and confident, knowing that she only had to jump through this hoop before she made her dash to the airport and stepped on the plane. As a result, the answers had flowed and she felt she'd done well.

"Yeah, metatarsal," the student in front agreed. And straight away a gaggle of girls gathered to discuss details of the answers they'd given.

Ashlee soon slipped away. She had a plane to catch, a game to win. She didn't have time to wonder if she'd secured a place at the school.

Instead, she hit the street and walked swiftly up Ninth Avenue to take a subway train from the Lincoln Centre all the way south and across the east River to downtown Brooklyn, and from there to JFK. The train rattled along the tracks, sliding through brightly lit stations, whooshing through dark tunnels.

Throughout the journey Ashlee kept her gaze on the floor, making no eye contact with her fellow passengers, hardly noticing the stations they passed through. She thought of Marissa and her parents negotiating the streets above, heading for the same airport, and then of her mom waiting tables right this minute at La Sila.

I've got to call her before I get on the plane, Ashlee reminded herself.

But when she reached her destination she had to concentrate on finding the right terminal, keeping tight hold of her bag and looking as though she was the kind of kid used to taking long plane journeys alone.

Two o'clock. Check in for Miami at Gate 54. Ashlee stood on the moving walkway, listening to the announcement echoing around every corner of the airport. She remembered the call home. Then she realised her mom would hear the announcements in the background. There was no way she could call her from the airport.

Fifteen minutes later, she had gone through the American Airlines check-in procedure. Her bag had been labelled and had vanished up the conveyor belt. Ashlee kept up the appearance that she did this all the time and explained to the check-in attendant that her dad would be meeting her at the other end. He checked her in as an unaccompanied minor, insisting that her mom really should have filled in the paperwork in advance.

"Um . . . I came with friends," she said quickly, as he looked around with a perplexed expression.

Straggling behind the attendant and his small group of people needing assistance, Ashlee quietly made her way to the gate.

The attendant had his hands full, so he nodded to Ashlee to go ahead on her own once they reached the gate. She got in line, showed the flight attendant her boarding pass and walked onto the plane.

Don't be flashy. Be tough. Hustle. Throughout the flight Ashlee stared out of the window, down at the sunlit clouds. She ran through the things she needed to do to impress the judges. *Pass well. Keep possession. Make the big play.*

"Would you like something to drink?"the flight attendant asked.

She jerked her attention back to the here and now and asked for orange juice. The attendant smiled at her and Ashlee smiled back.

"Is someone meeting you at the airport?" the man asked kindly.

She nodded. "My dad." *I hope. I pray!*

The middle-aged woman in the seat next to her saw this as an invitation to a personal conversation. "Hi, I'm Mary Kay. Are you on vacation? Does your dad live in Florida? I have a daughter in Sanibel. She just split from her husband. She has two little kids. Lord knows what's going to happen with the house!"

At last, after what seemed like an entire century, the pilot announced that they'd begun their descent.

Let me out of here! Ashlee thought. Mary Kay had just started in on the crimes the son-in-law had committed to break up the marriage. "He was never home. He never helped with the kids. Golf is his thing. He thinks he's Tiger Woods, but he ain't!"

The plane landed and bumped along the runway, engines whining. The outside temperature was a sunny 89 degrees, the pilot told them.

OK, Dad, don't let me down! Ashlee thought.

She filed out of the plane and boarded

the shuttlebus which lurched across the tarmac to the terminal.

I must be crazy! Ashlee thought. Her mouth was dry. The heat hit her as she stepped out of the bus and walked into the building. *Of course Dad will let me down. That's what he does!*

Once they reached the baggage claim, Ashlee assured the attendant that she would be fine and her dad would be right outside. Her bag was heavy as she lifted it off the carousel. People elbowed her out of the way. But she made it through the Arrivals door, into a sea of smiling faces and guys holding up placards to greet business travellers.

Ashlee looked from face to face. If her dad was in the crowd, he would stand head and shoulders above the others – but no, there was no tall ex-basketball player with blue eyes and thinning blonde hair. Her heart thudded and her hopes sank.

Gradually the meeters and greeters

found their passengers and the crowd melted away. There was still no sign of Ashlee's dad. She gazed beyond the airport building at the line of taxis and the blue sky beyond, blinking back the tears of disappointment.

Yeah, he's let you down big time. It's his speciality.

Lost in a fog of misery, Ashlee walked slowly across the empty marble floor. She had no idea where she was headed and didn't see the tall figure dressed in a black T-shirt and faded jeans cut across the vast space and come up alongside her.

"Hey," her dad said in that quiet voice that sounded like it didn't fit his size.

Ashlee gasped and dropped her bag. She didn't fling her arms around his neck and hug him the way another daughter might hug her dad.

"What's up? You look like you saw a ghost." He took the bag and led the way to the car park, not walking but loping.

Ashlee noted other people glancing, then staring. Did they recognize him from way back, or was it just his height that drew their attention? She half ran to keep up. "Thanks for sending me the tickets. This means a lot."

"Sure, no problem. Good to hear you made the camp." So quiet, so laid back he almost fell over. Slinging the bag into the back of a beat-up Jeep, he motioned Ashlee towards the passenger seat. "How's your mother?" he asked as he turned the key in the ignition.

"Good. How's Karen?"

"Karen's history."

"Since when?"

"Since November." Robert left the car park and hit the freeway. The low sun dazzled.

Karen had been her dad's long-time girlfriend – the one he'd left Theresa for. "How come?"

He shrugged. "You know."

"So why didn't you write and tell me?"

Getting personal stuff out of her father was like getting blood from a stone. Come to think of it, this was most likely where she got her own shyness from.

"And give your mom the satisfaction of saying 'I told you so!'" he said with a laugh. "I don't think so." Then he glanced sideways at her. "You look good."

"You too." His hair was cropped short, he was in decent shape. "Did you stop drinking?"

"'My name's Robert and I'm an alcoholic,'" he said, quoting the Alcoholics Anonymous line. "Yeah, I joined AA. I haven't touched a drink for eighteen months."

"Dad, that's cool!" This was more than cool – it was too good to believe. "I wish you'd told me."

There was a silence between them as Robert drove his car along a waterside area where white boats were moored. The houses were the stuff of lifestyle magazines.

"I got a job," he told her. "I work on the

maintenance team at the Golden Palm Golf Resort."

"Cool," she murmured. No girlfriend, no alcohol and one steady job. Wow!

"They give me a house, rent free. This is it," he announced, turning off the freeway and driving through the wide gates of the golf club. "The place isn't so hot, but it's got a spare room for you. Come on, take a look."

Ashlee's dad's miraculous transformation didn't include the ability to cook, so they sent out for pizza and settled down to eat it in front of the TV.

It was true – the place wasn't cosy. The walls were bare and the furniture simple. There was a worn rug on the floor.

"So tell me about you and the Tribeca Saints," Robert invited, to the background sounds of reality TV.

"What's to tell?" Ashlee put her feet up on the low table and bit into her pizza crust. "I'm the starting point-guard. My coach thinks I can make it to the top."

"You know it's tough," her dad warned. "It's a dog-eat-dog world up there."

"But you did it," she pointed out. How weird was it to be sitting here eating pizza, discussing her basketball future with her dad, when six days ago he didn't feature anywhere in her life.

"That's my point," he said quietly. "Sure, I was a good player. I had the talent. But there were always young guys snapping at my heels, wanting to take my place. You begin to feel the pressure, and the second that happens, you're dead meat."

"How come?"

"When you feel the pressure, your confidence goes," he explained. He too had his legs stretched out and his feet on the table. "You need to take the edge off that, and in my case I thought I could do it by having a drink the night before a big game."

"Then one drink turns to two, then three . . ." Ashlee said quietly. "And anyhow, it doesn't work."

Robert frowned. "Right," he muttered, getting up to make hot chocolate. "You grew up fast," he added with a shake of his head.

"I just took a scholarship exam for Queensbridge High School," she said, backing off from the intense look he gave her. "Mom wants me to be a doctor."

Robert nodded. "How about you?"

The answer came back quick and sure. "I want to play basketball."

"So you kept up the tactic of not telling Theresa that you flew down here for this camp?" Reading between the lines, he could see what she'd been up to.

Ashlee shook her head then looked at her watch. "Oh shoot, I was meant to call. But it's too late!"

"Do it tomorrow," her dad advised. "Get a good night's sleep. If you plan to play well in the trials, you're going to need it."

CHAPTER 6

This was the day that could change her life.

Ashlee woke up to bright sun and the clunk of the ancient air-conditioning unit in her dad's spare room. For a few seconds she was hazy about where she was.

"What do you want to eat for breakfast?" Her dad's knock on the door brought her round.

"Nothing, thanks."

"Yeah, that'll be bacon, hash browns and two eggs over easy," he insisted.

"Ew!" Right now she felt she couldn't eat a thing. But she showered and got dressed, then went to join him in the tiny kitchen. The smell of bacon cooking got her digestive juices working.

"OK, your coach back home gave you all the ground rules, right? Did she tell you the one thing that will mark you out from the rest in basketball is one hundred and ten percent effort and hard work?" It seemed Robert planned on serving advice along with breakfast.

"Yeah, Dad."

"And hustle!" he insisted. "Don't ever be nice on the floor. Drop the ladylike stuff and get in there."

"OK, I got that," Ashlee agreed, scooping hash browns into her mouth.

Robert insisted on setting off early to drive her to the try-out facilities. During the journey Ashlee unzipped her bag three times to make sure she had everything she needed. "These are my lucky shoes," she told her dad, pulling out her Air Jordans. "I wore them last week when we beat Brooklyn."

"Ah, I had some lucky shoes too. Scored me 30 points once against the Lakers." He parked his old Jeep next to the entrance to the gym.

Ashlee grinned. How great was this? Her dad, the ex-pro, not only handing out the advice, but also understanding the importance of lucky shoes. "Oops!" she muttered, remembering something. She dived into her pocket for her mobile phone, then called her mom's phone. "Better late than never," she told her dad with a shrug.

But the number rang out and went to voicemail.

Next Ashlee tried the apartment number. The same thing happened. "Weird," she whispered. "But I guess it's early. Maybe Mom's still in bed."

"Come on, move it," her dad urged. "Let's get in there ahead of the others, show the judges your work ethic."

★ ★ ★

Despite her dad's super-keenness, Ashlee found she wasn't the only one in the changing room. Marissa was there, lacing up her shoes, already changed into jogging pants and T-shirt.

She looked up and squealed with delight when she saw Ashlee. "This is so cool! Can you believe it?"

Ashlee grinned and shook her head. "I know. We made it this far. And guess what – my dad actually showed up at the airport!" She told Marissa about the job and the house. "He really cleaned up his act. And another thing – he's going to be out there today watching me play!"

"Oh, cool!" Marissa was truly happy for her friend. She waited while Ashlee got changed, then they went along the corridor to the gym arm-in-arm.

"Dad keeps on with the work-work-work stuff," Ashlee reported.

"With my dad it's the 'Be a team player' thing."

"Yeah, but don't be too nice, remember!"

"And always look for the open shot!" Marissa swapped parental advice with Ashlee and giggled. Their spirits were high, even if their stomachs were tied in nervous knots. They entered the gym to see Marissa's parents and Ashlee's dad hanging out together in the stands.

"Ashlee, how come you never told me your dad was *the* Robert Elkin?" Marissa's dad demanded, hailing them from across the floor. "He was only one of the highest scorers ever for Miami Heat!"

Ashlee's dad spread his hands and shrugged modestly. He towered over Marissa's parents.

"No one ever asked me," Ashlee replied.

"You're both way too modest," Marissa's mom protested. She turned to Robert. "What I always say about your girl is that she's a shy little mouse until you get her on the basketball court. Then she turns into a tiger!"

Ashlee's dad grinned. "I can't wait to

see that!"

Blushing to the roots of her blonde hair, Ashlee dragged Marissa away. They picked up two balls and began a gentle dribbling drill to warm up.

"Ash, I like your dad. He's cool," Marissa whispered as they dribbled to the baseline, pivoted and started back the way they'd come.

Ashlee dodged two other players who were warming up, glanced towards her father and grunted. She felt something she'd never felt before fight for space inside her chest. What was it? Pride – yeah, pride! She was proud of her dad, the basketball star, washed up at 35, but now with his life back on track and still remembered as a great player.

"Yeah," she agreed with Marissa. "He's cool. Now let's get out there and show the judges what we can do!"

"Hi, my name is Cissy Warner." A top

coach was introducing herself to the roster of players brought together for the Development Camp. "I'll be running practice this morning."

Eighty girls prepared to impress the judges. They came from every corner of the United States, from grey urban jungles and wide open prairies, from the golden coast of California to the rocky fishing ports of New England. Each one wore a numbered bib over her shirt and was prepared to do whatever she had to do to join the elite squad. They would go forward to compete for a place in the Junior National Team.

"I want this so much!" Marissa whispered to Ashlee.

"Me too," Ashlee confessed. She adjusted the number 6 bib and fixed her sights on gaining a treasured place for Puerto Rico in the summer.

"Choose a partner who you don't know," Cissy Warner instructed. "One player takes free throws; the other rebounds. Then switch. Okay, go!"

Shoot, rebound, pass. Ashlee and her partner – a girl called Erlana who was even taller and more athletic than she was – executed the drill perfectly. They settled into the rhythm and played gracefully and accurately. At the end of 20 shots, Ashlee felt at ease.

Erlana chose her again for the next drill, which was a defensive shuffle drill. No balls were needed – this was all to do with footwork and balance. Ashlee crouched and slid her feet sideways with quick, short steps, never letting Erlana move more than a foot away, though her opponent swerved, twisted and ran to escape. Then they switched roles.

"Good work, number 6!" Cissy picked out Ashlee and praised her speed.

Erlana frowned and took it as an insult to her own ability. She hopped and lunged at Ashlee, losing her balance and ending up on the ground. Ashlee offered a hand to help her up.

Next they changed partners and went on through a passing drill, then at last on to jump shots, where Ashlee knew she could excel. Sure enough, she scored all five short-range shots and only missed one jumper from outside. She saw the judges making notes on her performance and urged Marissa on to join her in the top-scoring group. Marissa too did well, only missing two shots.

"OK, take a break," Cissy instructed after 45 minutes of non-stop drills.

Ashlee and Marissa trotted over to their parents, who offered drinks and encouragement.

"How's it going?" Marissa's mom asked anxiously.

"Good," Marissa said, taking deep breaths then drinking thirstily.

Ashlee looked at her dad and waited for his judgment. It was the first time he'd ever seen her play and suddenly his opinion meant everything to her.

Robert pushed out his bottom lip and gazed at her through narrowed eyes.

"Well?" she whispered. The years of constant practice and tough competition fell away. She felt like a raw beginner in front of him. 'How did I do?'

There was a long silence that seemed to last forever. Robert's eyes didn't flicker. "Girl, you can play this game," he said at last, totally serious, without the hint of a smile. "Whatever the secret is, you've got it."

Ashlee breathed a sigh of relief. "Thanks, Dad!"

He smiled at last. "Go out there, Ashlee, and make me proud!"

After the break the judges asked the coach to split the girls into sixteen teams. The teams would play each other in a knockout tournament, each game lasting just ten minutes. After two rounds, the surviving four teams would go through to semi-finals that afternoon that would last twenty minutes, followed by the finals which would be open to the public and played the next day.

"Number 6, join the blue team!"

Ashlee heard her number called and found herself playing alongside Erlana, plus three other players named Lydia, Darcie and Lorene. Straight away Erlana put herself in charge, making herself point guard and pushing Ashlee to small forward, a position she wasn't familiar with.

OK, I'm fine with that, Ashlee decided. She went into the first game with her confidence high, eager to show what she could do.

The Blues were playing the Greens, who won the first tip-off and carried the ball down the court to score an early basket. A quick steal and lay-up by the Greens' number 22, and Ashlee's team began to fall behind quickly.

But Ashlee made sure she was part of the action the next time down the court, calling for the ball from Lydia and streaking towards the basket, marked by the Greens' number 40. Then she passed swiftly to Erlana at the top of the key. Erlana aimed and shot, scoring two points for the Blues. They were off and on a roll, gaining possessions and running circles around the opposition until the referee called Lorene for a blocking foul.

Ashlee watched the Green team slowly edge back into the game. She saw their strong number 22 free herself from Erlana and position herself for a shot. Quick as a flash, Ashlee darted in and intercepted the pass.

"Go, Ashlee!" A voice rose from the small crowd of parents and supporters.

Ashlee dribbled, swerved and dodged. She recognized her dad's voice cheering her. Boosted by his belief in her, she faked, twisted and freed herself up to shoot. She leaped high in the air. With a flick of her wrist, she scooped the ball up and into the hoop.

Those were just two of the fifteen points she scored in the game. The Blues beat the Greens by 24 points to 12.

"Good, but watch your number 15," Ashlee's dad warned during the break between games. Other teams had taken to the court. The action was fast and furious.

"You mean Erlana?" Ashlee checked.

"Yeah, your point guard. She's trying to freeze you out of the action."

"Why would she do that?" Marissa cut in. "Ashlee's the best player in the Blue team."

"That's why," Robert explained. "Erlana's a selfish player. She doesn't want Ashlee's ability to shine through. You take a good hard look during the next game."

"Listen to your dad," Marissa's mom told Ashlee. "He knows what he saying!"

"OK, it's Oranges versus Reds." Marissa's dad clapped to gain their attention. "Marissa, you're out there."

"Good luck!" Ashlee hissed as Marissa ran onto the floor.

Eight teams came through the first round, including Marissa's Reds and Ashlee's Blues. They went into round two knowing that everything still depended on putting on an exceptional show of strength and speed.

Robert took Ashlee to one side before she stepped out on to the floor to play the Yellows. "This is important. Don't let Erlana steal the glory," he reminded her. "You find your own way to that basket."

Ashlee frowned. It was weird to be vying with a member of her own team – something she'd never had to do before. But she knew her dad was right. Erlana's strong willpower was in danger of unbalancing the team.

Meanwhile, Erlana stalked out ahead of

her, arranging with the rest of the team to set up the offense, putting herself forwrrad as the primary scorer. "Ashlee, you play from the wing," she insisted. "Feed me the passes I need to score the points."

Who made you Numero Uno? Ashlee thought with a frown. But Darcie and Lydia seemed happy to be guided by Erlana.

"Hey, Ashlee, where are you from?" Lydia asked as they waited for the officials to take their positions.

"Tribeca Saints – New York. How about you?"

"I live here in Florida. Cissy Warner is my full-time coach."

"Wow!" Ashlee's eyebrows shot up. It seemed Lydia already had at least one foot through the door to Puerto Rico.

"Darcie's too," Lydia added. "We both play for Orlando Magic Juniors."

Ashlee took a deep breath and tried hard to keep her confidence boosted to its top notch. Around here everyone you spoke to sounded as if they were aiming to psych the other person out.

"But not me," Lorene told Ashlee with a grin. She had a wide, open face and short curly brown hair. "I'm from Indiana, smack in the middle of nowhere in particular. No one even knows my name."

"So let's show these Florida kids," Ashlee grinned back as the whistle went. She and Lorene were the outsiders, but they would show they were as good as the rest.

Not simply as good, but better! Lorene passed to Ashlee and Ashlee found the space. She cut through to score – once, twice, three times.

"You're not running the plays," Erlana hissed. "We had a game plan, remember?"

It didn't matter. The score was Blues 13, Yellows 3.

Erlana crossed over the half-court line and passed to Darcie. Darcie blundered straight into a Yellow defender, lost possession and was left flat-footed with the ball careening towards the sideline.

A Yellow defender dived to the floor to recover the loose ball. Ashlee did the same, wrestled the ball away, and threw a spectacular bounce-pass to Lorene from the ground. Erlana yelled for a pass and then used her strength to dribble past the two opponents.

She was outside the key, preparing to shoot, but she was off balance and her shot ricocheted off the rim. Erlana shot and missed. She turned to blame Lorene for a weak pass.

Ashlee saw the judges scribble notes and talk amongst themselves. *How do they see things*, she wondered.

But she wasn't distracted for long. The ball was in play again and soon the Yellows had narrowed the gap. Lydia had committed a turn over, opening up a gap for the Yellow team to take advantage and score. Then there was another error, this time from Lorene.

OK, we need something special here, Ashlee decided during a timeout. It was clear that Erlana was doing exactly what her dad had warned her about and was freezing her out of the game. But would the judges spot that? Or would they write Ashlee off as a second-rate player, unable to hold her own in this talented company?

No way! The thought made Ashlee super-determined. She took Lorene to one side. "We have to speed things up," she told her urgently. "Erlana is trying to hold the pace back and use her strength, but it's not working. My idea is to pick up the pace. We can outrun them. Do you think we can do it?"

Lorene nodded. The referee's whistle called them back onto the floor.

And now it was all or nothing for Ashlee and Lorene. At every chance they got, they stole possession, quickly pushed the ball up the court, and sprinted for all they were worth.

"Yeah, Ashlee!" Robert yelled from the sideline. "Take it to the hoop! You go, girl!"

Ashlee's long legs carried her at top speed. She glanced around, knowing that she couldn't pass back to Erlana, who was struggling to keep up. No, she had to go solo for the points, faking past the last defender, leaping and twisting in mid-air towards the basket.

"Amazing!" Marissa's mom and dad clapped and yelled.

Robert stood and said nothing, a smile splitting his face from ear to ear.

"I swear she's a star in the making!" Marissa's dad cheered.

Ashlee was pushing for victory, playing for all she was worth.

CHAPTER 7

At lunchtime Ashlee showered before she went to the café to meet her dad. Marissa chatted non-stop through the cubicle wall.

"Who do the Blues play in the semi?" she wanted to know.

"The Whites. Did you watch them play this morning?"

"Yeah, they're good," Marissa replied. "Reds play the Blacks. They have one player who's way ahead of the rest. If we can close her out and keep possession, I reckon we'll come out on top. Hey Ash, you handled your pushy team-mate pretty well out there in your last match. Good for you."

"Thanks." Ashlee was glad she'd taken her dad's advice and had been able to show the judges her top game. After all, that was why she was there. "Listen, I have to run. Dad's waiting for me."

Dad's waiting for me. The phrase sounded unfamiliar but good on her lips.

"Yeah, cool. I'll see you in the dining area," Marissa called from under the shower.

So Ashlee dressed and hurried on. But out in the passageway she forgot which way to turn and found herself skirting past steam rooms and saunas and through a maze of corridors, trying to find a sign for the restaurant. She noted one for the swimming pool, then for the tennis courts – no, she still wasn't going in the right direction. She decided to try following signs for the exit and start again. Sighing, she hurried on.

At last she made it to the main foyer at the front of the sports complex, where there was a large board with a plan of the whole building. *I'm right here*, Ashlee thought, tracing with her forefinger the route she should take to the dining area. Just then, she sensed someone come close up behind her and invade her space. Irritated, she glanced over her shoulder, then jumped with fright.

"Yeah, it's me," her mom said quietly, staring her straight in the eyes.

Ashlee gasped. "What are you doing here?"

"Following you."

"How come? How . . . Oh jeez!' For a few seconds Ashlee was disorientated. As far as she had known, her mom was waiting tables in New York. Was this some kind of trick? But no – here was Theresa in the flesh, scraped-back dark hair escaping in wisps around her thin face, looking pale and stern.

"I suppose you want to know how I found out," her mom went on, ignoring a crowd of kids who had arrived to watch the afternoon semi finals. "It's actually down to the fact that you didn't call me like you promised."

Ashlee closed her eyes tight and hung her head. "Yeah Mom, I'm sorry about that."

"I called Marissa's house. There was no one home."

Ashlee nodded, unable to look up. She couldn't meet Theresa's eyes.

"At which point I smelled a rat. And guess what – I checked my phone messages and, surprise, there was one from Erika Schrader wishing you luck in Miami."

"Oh no!" Ashlee groaned.

Her mom went on relentlessly in a flat, deliberate voice. "So I called your precious coach and she told me all about Florida and the basketball camp. I was speechless. She was totally shocked that you'd never informed me. I put down the phone and bought the first plane ticket I could find. I flew down this morning."

"I'm sorry!" Ashlee said helplessly and

inadequately. This was why her mom hadn't answered the phone – she'd been 36,000 feet up in the air. *Nightmare! Total meltdown!*

"You take a plane down the length of the country without telling me." Theresa pointed out the obvious. "You lie to me about studying in the library, when all the time you're skipping your work and throwing some stupid ball around a basketball court!"

"Mom!" As Theresa's voice rose and strangers began to stare, Ashlee backed into the women's bathroom.

"You blew it, Ashlee! You neglected your studies and you defied me."

"I know. I'm sorry." No, the repetition of the "S" word simply didn't cover it.

"For a game – a stupid game!" Theresa protested. "When you had the best chance of getting that scholarship. How could you be so stupid?"

"I went to Queensbridge and did the test," Ashlee told her. She was backed up against the washbasins, fighting the tears. "I think I did OK."

"OK is not good enough. There are a hundred others who will do better than OK. You needed to work, to give it all your concentration." Theresa's eyes were filling up too. Her lips trembled as she continued to attack her daughter.

"Mom, you were asking me to do the impossible." Weakly Ashlee tried to defend herself. "I want to play basketball. I can't give it up."

"Oh, and basketball is going to put food on your table and keep a roof over your head for the rest of your life!" Theresa scoffed.

OK, enough! Theresa didn't have to say it out loud – Ashlee knew that Theresa had directed this last remark against her dad, whose career had gone into freefall. He hadn't provided the food or the roof since Ashlee was six years old. Suddenly she couldn't take any more. "Let me out of here!" she cried, pushing her mom aside and heading for the exit.

But at that moment the door opened and a kid in a tracksuit came in, closely followed by another, then by Marissa's mother.

"Hey, Theresa!" Marissa's mom said, bright and cheery. "Great to see you. Glad you could make it." Noticing the look of Theresa's face, she slowed down and trailed off.

"Hello, Susan." Ashlee's mom took a deep breath and almost succeeded in putting on a normal act.

But Ashlee needed to get out of the enclosed space before her head exploded. She made a dash for the door.

"The girls are doing just great," Susan went on awkwardly. "They're both through to the semis of the knockout competition, and of course Robert is giving Ashlee the best advice . . ."

"Robert?" Theresa frowned.

Ashlee stopped, her hand outstretched,

reaching for the door. *Oh no!*

Susan took a sharp intake of breath. "Ashlee's dad. Well, of course, why am I telling *you* that? All I'm saying is, it's wonderful for Ashlee to have a professional player backing her up . . ." Once more she faltered.

"Robert is here?" Theresa asked faintly, looking from Susan to Ashlee with eyes like a stricken deer's.

Susan struggled back into action, trying to ease things. "Yes, I thought you knew."

"You contacted him?" Theresa whispered, sliding between Ashlee and the door and confronting her.

Ashlee nodded, petrified. She'd gone and broken her mother's heart!

"He sent you the plane tickets in the envelope you hid from me?"

She nodded again. Yes, she'd smashed Theresa's heart into tiny pieces.

"Oh, Ashlee!" her mom sighed.

Theresa opened the door and walked

away, right through the reception area, out into the heat of the sun.

"But Ash, your mom puts way too much pressure on you," Marissa soothed. "You always have to be the best in every possible way."

"Dragon Mom!" Ashlee smiled faintly. But inside she was torn apart.

It was after lunch. They were sitting with Marissa's mom and dad in the stadium, waiting for the judges to arrive. Robert had gone looking for Theresa to try and calm her down.

"I'm sure she was only thinking of what was best for you," Susan put in. Mrs Peacemaker, the apple-pie mom.

"If I'd been in your shoes, I would've done the same thing," Marissa insisted. "I wouldn't give up basketball if you paid me a million dollars!"

"I wonder where she went," Ashlee said. What with her mom's broken heart and her own exploding head, the issue of playing in the semis had somehow taken a back seat.

But her dad had insisted she should play. No – what Robert had actually said when Marissa's mom had taken her sobbing from the bathroom and found him in the dining area was: "You get out there, girl, and kick serious butt!"

She'd quietened down at last and tried to tell him she couldn't focus, that this was a crisis she couldn't sideline, but he'd cut her short and gone to look for Theresa.

Now, to her surprise, it was Marissa's suit-wearing businessman dad who helped her. "This isn't your problem, Ashlee," he said quietly as the judges took their places and the stadium filled with spectators. "This is really a problem between your mom and dad."

They all stared at him, then Marissa nodded. "What did I tell you?"

"You do what you have to do and don't

get caught in the middle," her dad insisted. "Let the adults fix up their own mess."

The White team strode onto the court like they were winners. They held their heads high and took up position for the start of the game.

Erlana led the Blues out. "Let's play the same offence as last game. I'll keep playing point."

Lorene disagreed. "Put Ashlee in the attack," she insisted. "She's the fastest player we have."

"Yeah, that's true." Lydia broke ranks. At this point, all she cared about was winning. Erlana could think what she liked. "Erlana, you're strong by the basket. You should play power forward."

So that's the way it worked, with Ashlee jumping high to win the tip-off and passing straight to Lorene, who dribbled neatly and swiftly towards the basket. Ashlee dashed to the hoop, received the "give and go", and instinctively pulled up to shoot and score the first points.

Lorene and Lydia slapped her on the back.

Now, after a slow start, the Whites came alive, running a series of clever plays to get past the Blues' defence. The score was tied. Each and every player stretched every muscle in their bodies to put their team ahead.

At the end of ten minutes, they broke for halftime. Ashlee was breathing hard, listening to Erlana take charge of tactics for the second half.

"Slow it down," Erlana insisted. "Keep possession. Don't take risks."

Bad advice! Ashlee thought. "Why go into defensive mode?" she objected. "The game is still too close to call. We need to be out there on the attack."

Just then she was distracted by a tall figure striding down the raked steps towards the front of the crowd. It was her dad, coming back alone. There was no sign of her mom.

"I'll be right back," she told her team-mates, sprinting across the floor towards him.

"Ashlee, we need to go over our game plan for the second half!" Erlana called loudly after her, making the judges in the box turn their heads and stare.

"So?" Ashlee demanded. "Did you find Mom? What did she say?"

Robert shook his head. "She disappeared. Sorry."

Ashlee felt her heart jolt. "I really let her down, didn't I?"

Her dad scratched his head. "I guess you should have told her. Or I should. But it's too late now."

Sighing, Ashlee threw back her head and stared up at the rows of bright lights. *OK, get a grip. Don't ruin this chance. Go back out there and play!*

"Go!" her dad urged.

The referee blew her whistle and the

teams took their positions for the final ten minutes.

"You OK?" Lorene asked Ashlee. "You look kind of shaky."

"I'm fine," Ashlee insisted. She took a deep breath and tried to concentrate.

At the start of the second half the Whites came out quickly. Before the Blues knew it, a White player had shot and scored.

"Whoo, good job!" The White team bundled together and gave each other high fives. Then they jogged back into position, ready to do the same thing all over again.

We need something new! Ashlee decided. She felt the game beginning to slip away, saw Erlana yelling at Lorene and Lydia, taking out her frustration. *We are taking too many jump shots. We have to work inside and drive through to the hoop!*

This time, when Darcie passed to Ashlee, she pivoted on the spot and faked a shot, drawing the defender. Ashlee then dribbled on a fast diagonal sprint towards the key. She was through and free to shoot.

The crowd watched Ashlee's split-second dodges and swerves. They saw her lose two opponents and hardly pause at the key.

Whoosh! The ball flew through the air in a high arc. It dropped swift and true through the hoop, touching nothing but net.

Ashlee jumped up and punched the air. Her team-mates gathered to congratulate her. The Blues were back in the game; their hopes were up.

But then, as Ashlee ran back to play defence, she spotted a movement behind the judges' box and saw with horror that her mom was walking down the stadium steps towards her dad.

Then it was as if everything went into slow motion – the signals from the officials, the other players loping into position. Her mom walked right up to her dad, jabbed her finger into his chest and mouthed words that were impossible to hear.

Ashlee let out a long breath, like a balloon deflating. It was as if her ribcage had caved in and it was impossible to take another breath.

"You OK?" Lorene checked again.

In the distance, Theresa yelled and jabbed at Robert. Marissa's dad tried to step in between them. The referee blew her whistle.

Ashlee nodded and blindly punched the ball clear from the Whites' oncoming point guard. Lorene recovered it and dribbled towards the Blues' basket, with a White defender following closely behind. It was her turn to shine – she came to a sudden stop and faked. The defender flew by her, allowing Lorene to toss the ball off the backboard and in, scoring two vital points.

Ashlee closed her eyes tight, opened them and looked into the crowd. Marissa's dad was still standing in the aisle, staring up the steps. Robert was slumped in a seat. There was no sign of Theresa.

Whites 31, Blues 29.

The Blues were losing and Ashlee's parents were engaged in World War Three.

"Ashlee, get into position!" Erlana bellowed.

She sucked in a deep breath and made her lungs and legs work again. OK, so this was as hard as things got. So did she have it – the mental toughness that Erika had questioned, that Robert had said she needed? Could she be like Michael Jordan, who loved the game so much that he overcame all barriers and found a way to win?

The whistle blew. The ball came at Ashlee like a rocket. She caught it with both hands and wove between her opponents. She saw the hoop way ahead, many bodies in between. She dribbled first with her right hand, then her left. A defender slide-stepped and tried to close her out, but Ashlee was too lithe, too fast. Now there was no one between her and the basket. Springing into the air, Ashlee reached towards the basket, finger-rolling the ball into the hoop.

"Go, Ashlee, kiss the rim!" Marissa shouted, both arms in the air, cheering her friend.

Kiss it like you love the moment. Rejoice in that split-second when victory falls within your grasp.

CHAPTER 8

The sun set that night over the lake at the Golden Palm Golf resort, its pink rays reflected in the smooth water.

"So," Robert said to Ashlee as they walked along beside the lake, "you and Marissa both got to where you wanted to be."

The Blues and the Reds had won their semi finals. They were through to the final where they would play against each other.

"It doesn't feel that way," Ashlee sighed. After the sweet taste of victory came the guilt. "I can't get Mom out of my head. I lied to her. I mean, what kind of person does that make me?"

"Normal," her dad pointed out. "It's

your mom who's way out of line."

"Really?" Ashlee stopped to look at the view. The green, flat sweep of the empty golf course spread into the distance.

"Yeah, she totally lost it back there in the stadium. When she was yelling at me, she wasn't thinking about you and how it would affect your performance – she was only thinking of herself."

"But . . ." Ashlee tried to put into words the complicated thoughts running through her head. "I can't believe I'm actually saying this, but Dad, maybe Mom's right – there are more important things than basketball . . . maybe?"

As her voice rose and ended in a question mark, Robert acted shocked. "Hey, that's my religion you're talking about!"

"Dad, be serious! I feel bad. What did Mom say to you?"

"Nothing. The same as always. Everything's down to me – I'm the one who taught you how to lie and cheat, yack–yack–yack."

"Ouch!" Turning from the water, Ashlee retraced their steps towards his house. "You know she turned off her cell phone again?"

"Yeah, the silent treatment. That's so you feel extra bad."

"Well it works," she muttered, shaking her head. "Do you think maybe she flew back to New York?"

"Don't ask me. Look, she knows you're safe, that's the main thing. And she knows you had to keep stuff from her in order to achieve your dream. What she does now is up to her."

End of conversation. Her dad made it clear he didn't want to talk about his ex-wife any more. Instead he advised Ashlee to chill out, then get a good night's sleep. "It's a big day tomorrow," he reminded her.

"Huge," she agreed.

As they strolled into the house, he put his arm around her shoulder. "Things have moved pretty fast these last twenty-four hours, Ash. I want you to know how much it means to me."

She nodded. "Me too."

"Not just the game. Everything."

"I know, Dad."

"And don't worry about Theresa. She'll get used to stuff."

"Can I have hot chocolate?" Ashlee asked, breaking away and flopping down on the couch. Somehow she didn't see her mom ever coming round to the basketball point of view.

Not after what Ashlee and her dad had done. It was a trust thing. And the trust, like Theresa's heart, was broken.

It was long after midnight and Ashlee was still staring out of her window at the starry sky.

Her phone lay on the pillow next to her in case her mom called.

Maybe I should fly home and talk to her,

Ashlee thought. *I'm all she has. She must be hurting a lot.*

But the stars twinkled and seemed to remind her of her dream.

I have to be at the gym tomorrow, she told herself. *I worked so hard to reach the final, I can't throw it away.*

Ashlee picked up the phone and called Theresa one last time. As always, it went straight to her voicemail.

Sighing, she thought of all the days and nights her mom had worked at the restaurant. The days built up to weeks, months and long years – hard work for low pay, like crawling through a tunnel with no light at the end.

Yeah, no wonder she doesn't want that for me, Ashlee thought.

Yet for Theresa it had all been so different at the start – a glamorous young woman married to a high-earning basketball star, basking in the sunshine glow of fame and money.

Ashlee punched her pillow and tried to get comfortable. She turned over and tried again. It was no good.

That's it – I fly home early tomorrow morning! she concluded. She knew it was the biggest decision she'd ever taken and if anyone had asked her why she was giving up on the final and turning her back on her dream, she wouldn't have been able to put it into words. Only that the certainty welled up from deep inside and lodged in her brain.

I have to fly home and talk to Mom. Don't ask. Don't try to stop me. This is something I have to do!

"I understand," Robert said quietly.

"You do?" Everything about this sudden reversal took Ashlee by surprise – her own decision, her dad's reaction, the fact that she didn't feel torn in two any longer.

Calmly they faced each other over the narrow breakfast bar. 'I see what you're doing and why you're doing it," he insisted, determined to hide his own disappointment. "It's a major thing to pull out of this camp but I'm backing you, Ashlee, whatever you choose."

"Thanks, Dad."

"Try again next year," he suggested calmly. "Don't let your talent go to waste."

"Like you did?" Suddenly nothing was out of bounds. She felt she could talk to him about anything.

"Absolutely," he admitted, gazing out of the open door and across the fairway. "No one knows better than me that I had it all and I threw it away."

"You and Mom breaking up – who was to blame?"

"One hundred and ten percent me. I was drinking, my head was turned by the fame. Theresa gave me a dozen chances and I blew them all."

Ashlee looked down at her hands, silent.

"It's been hard for her," Robert

acknowledged. "My problem is, the moment I see her I go into a tailspin of guilt."

"Have you told her?"

He shook his head. "The second she sets eyes on me, she comes crashing down on me in a wave of anger. I don't get a chance. And I don't deserve one."

"I get it!" Ashlee muttered, more determined than ever to fly home and set things straight with her mom.

She packed her bag while Robert checked plane times. He said he would drive her straight to the airport.

"Not playing in the final?" Marissa repeated when Ashlee called her at her hotel. "Are you crazy?"

"I'll explain when you get back to New York," Ashlee said hurriedly. "Bye, and good luck in the final!"

She and Robert were putting her bags in his Jeep when a taxi pulled up outside the house and Ashlee's mom stepped out.

"There's no need to wait,"Theresa told the driver. She paid him and the car drove away.

For a while no one said a word. Ashlee stared at her mom, stunned.

"OK, OK," Theresa began, putting up both hands as if to ward off Ashlee's anger.

"We thought you'd gone home!" Ashlee cried. "You didn't answer your phone."

"I went back to my hotel. I needed to think."

"Mom, I pulled out of the final."

Theresa didn't react but rushed on. "I thought it through from every angle," she explained. "Mostly I thought about how much playing this game means to you, Ashlee. I never really gave that any space in my head before."

"I pulled out," Ashlee said again. Still she couldn't get through.

"For the first time I tried to imagine how it feels to be you," her mom went on. "I remembered when you were a little kid down here in Florida, how you ran around on the lawn, always with a basketball in your hands. You were so full of energy. And you grew up loving the game and, as you can imagine, that gave me a hard time."

"I know, Mom. I understand."

Theresa stood in the driveway in her jeans and T-shirt, small and vulnerable.

"Because you were so clever, always ahead of the other kids. So intelligent."

She shook her head, fighting the croak in her voice that came from tears building up inside her.

"Come inside and talk," Robert said. He led the way.

"OK, I'm good," Theresa insisted as Ashlee sat her down and Robert brought a glass of water. "What I realised when I worked it out last night in that miserable hotel room was that it was me – I got it all wrong."

Ashlee sat down opposite her and stared. For the first time her mom met her gaze. "It's not a straight choice, is it? I mean, it doesn't have to be basketball or the scholarship – one or the other."

"You mean it?" Ashlee gasped.

Theresa nodded. "It can be both."

"Yes!" Ashlee glanced round at her dad who was keeping a low profile by the door. After all these years, after all the fights, a door had finally opened inside her mom's heart.

"I know how hard you've worked to get here, and how hard you studied for Queensbridge. You've put in the effort to achieve what you want in life. Work hard, play hard," Theresa said with a shrug. "That way you can have it all!"

CHAPTER 9

A big crowd had gathered to watch the final of the US Women's Youth Basketball Camp. The gym buzzed with expectation.

"Can you see my mom?" Ashlee asked Marissa as they stood at the side of the floor, waiting for the judges to take their seats. "You're never going to believe this, but she's sitting next to Dad, just behind your folks – take a look!"

"You're right – I don't believe it!" Marissa gasped. The last time she had seen of the two of them, Theresa had been yelling at Robert, spoiling for a fight.

Ashlee grinned. "I know, it's incredible. I'll explain later."

"That's what you said before," Marissa

complained. "When you told me you were pulling out of the final."

"Sorry. Things happen fast," Ashlee laughed. She felt she was floating on air, free from all the pressures that had been pushing her down all her life. "Hey listen, the Blues are going to whup the Reds out there – you'll see!"

"How come you're trying to psych me out? I thought you were my friend?" Marissa complained, pretending to be upset. They pulled off their jogging pants and began warming up in their shorts.

"What's friendship got to do with it?" Ashlee replied with one last grin. They were here at last, about to play the biggest game of their lives. "This is the final, baby. This is war!"

The Blues against the Reds in the final. They were the elite of American youth basketball and they strutted their stuff out on the court. The tall, strong, graceful girls eased themselves into action with warm-up drills as the judges settled to their task.

Ashlee and Marissa worked together to stretch and practise some jump stops until Ashlee noticed Erlana glaring at her. "Oops, at this point it looks like I'd better stick with my team-mates," she muttered.

Marissa nodded and wished her luck. "But don't expect any favours from me!" she warned mock-seriously as Ashlee jogged back to the Blue half.

When she arrived, Erlana was in a huddle with Lydia and Darcie.

"What?" Ashlee asked, spreading her hands, palms upwards.

"We want to know how come you're so cosy with the Reds all of a sudden?" Darcie muttered.

Ashlee stared back in surprise. "It's not sudden. Marissa and I play in the Tribeca Saints together – back home in New York."

"That sounds pretty cosy to me," Erlana

said, as if her suspicions were confirmed. "Listen up, Ashlee. You don't act like a good team player and now I see why!"

"Hey!" Ashlee protested as Erlana turned her back and Darcie and Lydia muttered between themselves. "What does she see?" she asked Lydia.

Lydia gave her a straight answer. "She thinks you don't have the right team chemistry going with us. Erlana spotted that right from the start."

"But I do!" Ashlee couldn't believe what she was hearing. Then the obvious reason struck her between the eyes. "Look, don't trust Erlana. She's playing mind games. That's how much she wants to get on the judges' selection list!"

"As if!" Lydia and Darcie shook their heads in mocking disbelief and turned away.

OK, don't believe me! Ashlee thought.

But now she knew for sure that Erlana saw her as a major rival in this vital stage of the selection process. This last trick was just one more tactic to get Ashlee frozen out of the game.

"I'll show them who's the team player around here!" she said softly as the teams lined up for the tip-off.

Every girl played her best game. They moved like lightning, thought faster still, dribbling and passing, turning and faking like they were born to play basketball.

The crowd cheered basket after glorious basket and some superb defensive play as the ball whizzed from one end of the court to the other. They chanted their support and rose from their seats to celebrate whenever their team scored. Down in the judges' box, the watching adjudicators quietly noted their comments.

As self-elected point guard, Erlana was once more hogging the ball, deliberately freezing Ashlee out of offence and calling for the ball, even when she wasn't in a good position.

OK, I'll get in there and grab that ball for myself! Ashlee decided after the first five frustrating minutes of the game. The score was even at 9 points each. She quickly stole the ball and sprinted out onto the left wing. Coming up against two defensive Reds, she swiftly changed direction and cut through to the key.

Erlana was open on the other side of the court. Ashlee passed. Erlana shot and scored.

A cheer went up for the Blues. The crowd stamped their feet.

But almost before the Blues knew it, the Reds had won possession and were charging into their half. Swifter than the rest, Marissa sprinted ahead to the 3-point line, caught the pass, pivoted and scored.

This time the Reds' supporters went crazy and the gym erupted again.

Ashlee took a deep breath and glanced at the spot in the crowd where her mom and dad sat. They were on the edges of their seats, leaning forward. Another deep breath and Ashlee was ready to go.

This time Lorene swept a low bounce-pass out to Erlana on the Blues' 3-point line. But Marissa intercepted the pass, only to come up against a strong challenge from Ashlee.

"Go, Reds!" the supporters yelled.

Ashlee rushed towards Marissa, crouching low. Marissa faked but Ashlee didn't fall for it. Instead she kept up her challenge, forcing Marissa to pivot and look for help.

Then Erlana came in to double-team Marissa. Now she had to pass. She pivoted again and for a split-second Erlana roughly caught hold of her opponent's elbow.

The whistle blew. The referee signalled a foul for "reaching in".

The Red players set up their out-of-bounds play. The Blues were under pressure, thanks to Erlana's panicky foul. The crowd held their breath.

"Break!" shouted the inbounder, as she slapped back the ball.

The ball flew high over the heads of the players, towards Marissa, who was open for a split-second. Erlana and Ashlee both leaped high to knock the ball away. They collided in midair, and Ashlee felt a sharp pain in her ribs as both girls fell to the floor. Ashlee rolled onto her side and lay still.

The official signalled to stop the clock.

Ashlee lay there, unable to breathe. She'd taken a blow from Erlana's elbow – maybe her rib was cracked!

"Don't move," the referee warned, kneeling beside her. She shielded Ashlee from the other players who crowded round. In the background Erlana got to her feet and bent double, grabbing her leg as if her thigh was injured.

Ashlee lay with her knees drawn up to her chest. She was certain that Erlana's elbow jab had been deliberate.

How crazy is that! Her life's dream lay in pieces, thanks to a player from her own team!

Quickly the referee called for a physio for both injured players.

"Ash, are you OK?" Marissa ducked under the referee's arm. She hissed urgently at her injured friend. "Come on, try to stand up!"

"No, lie still," the physio advised, kneeling beside Ashlee. "Where does it hurt?"

"Between my ribs, here!"

"OK, you took a blow, the muscles are in spasm. Take your time. Try to breathe normally."

"Did she break a rib?" Marissa asked the physio anxiously.

Please God, no! Ashlee prayed. *Give me a fair chance to earn my place. This means everything to me!* Slowly she drew breath into her lungs and the pain eased. She rolled onto her back.

The physio nodded. "That's good.

Breathe deep."

Breathe. Relax. Breathe. Ashlee concentrated.

"Can you sit?" the physio asked.

"You bet." Ashlee sat and then stood up. The pain was ebbing. She was going to be OK.

Five yards away, Erlana was still bent double and refusing to look in Ashlee's direction.

Yeah, that was a dirty trick. Ashlee stood tall, ready to go. From now on she would keep well clear of Erlana and play her heart out to get selected.

The referee blew her whistle and raised her arm to restart the clock.

Wearing her lucky pair of Air Jordans, Ashlee sprinted and dodged. She jumped, shot and rebounded. She hustled for every pass, freed herself up and dribbled effortlessly down the length of the court.

"That girl is good!" members of the crowd agreed. Robert Elkin and Theresa

Carson sat with pride in their hearts.

Blues 24, Reds 22. Ashlee scored two more points, leaping high and punching the air.

The judges wrote their careful notes.

I love this game! Ashlee thought as she effortlessly scored another two points.

She ran, she ducked, she dodged. She had the vision to see ahead, forecast the opposition's next move and be there before them.

"Ashlee's got what it takes!" Theresa murmured to Robert, realizing for the very first time that her daughter's basketball star shone bright.

We're going to win! Ashlee swore as she nudged the Blues into a late lead. Blues 33, Reds 30.

She never considered the option of defeat.

CHAPTER 10

"These are the names of the players who will be going forward to the USA Junior National Trials in Mayaguez, Puerto Rico," the head judge announced.

The stadium was silent. Marissa sat with her mom and dad. Ashlee stood between Robert and Theresa. The lights overhead seemed to blur and float.

"In no particular order: Lydia Robinson, Florida; Christianne Barry, Texas; Marissa Roberts, New York."

Marissa gasped and hid her face behind her hands. Her mom and dad fell on her and hugged her until at last she emerged, her face showing total disbelief.

Ashlee looked up at the lights and

held her breath as the judge continued her announcement.

"Lorene Newby, Indiana; Ellen Carroll, Arizona; Leah Knight, California."

Six players had already been selected. Ashlee was not amongst them. She held her head high, listening, beginning to worry.

"Genifer Holby, Florida; Ashlee Carson, New York; Carolyn Harper . . ."

Ashlee's legs went weak and she collapsed into her seat. Her dad pulled her up and put his arms around her. Her mom jumped up and down on the spot.

"Yeah, baby!" Robert cried.

Ashlee wormed her way out of his embrace and hugged her mom. "I did it!" she cried. "Mom, did you see? I just got into the National Trials!"

"You were on fire!" Robert told Ashlee.

He had driven Theresa and Ashlee to a pizza place by the waterside, letting all the waiters know about his daughter's success as they were seated at their table.

"Yeah, well, knowing you and Mom were there definitely helped," Ashlee replied. "Besides, that kid from Florida got under my skin."

"Which one?" To Theresa, the whole match had been a blur of red and blue bibs, of whistles blowing and a tangle of long legs and arms.

"Erlana. She tried to keep me from even touching the ball."

"Yeah, what did I tell you?" Ashlee's dad waved at a couple of people across the room who had recognized him.

"Even after she stuck her elbow in my ribs, no way was I going to let her get the best of me," Ashlee grinned.

"She missed out on the selection," her dad pointed out. "What goes around comes around."

"But you were good!" Theresa said, as if still in a state of shock, staring at her bowl of pasta without touching it.

Robert and Ashlee exchanged looks and laughed.

"I mean, I knew from what I'd been told. But I guess I had to see it to believe."

"You'd better believe it," Robert insisted. "My girl is going to storm through to the national championship!"

"*Our* girl," Theresa said quietly.

They fell silent. The Carson-Elkins were never much good at talking and, though during this weekend things had changed faster than the speed of light, some things would always stay the same.

"So, Ashlee . . ." Theresa said as they sat together on the plane home.

"So, Mom?" Here it came – the lecture about lying and breaking trust. Ashlee had been waiting for it. She'd suspected her mom would save it until they were alone.

"I guess this is goodbye," Robert had said as he dropped them off at the Departures door. He'd left his car engine running in a restricted zone, arranging things so that the farewells were short and sweet. It was better that way.

"Yeah, Dad. Thanks." Ashlee had felt she would cry if he didn't leave right away.

"Thank you, Robert," Theresa had said, almost under her breath, but it in itself had been a small miracle.

Not that there was going to be an earth-shattering reconciliation between her parents – Ashlee hadn't fooled herself about that.

But her dad had a home and a job, and her mom had agreed to go out for a meal together and wasn't yelling at him. Her dad had asked Ashlee to text him when they landed back home. Hey, that was progress!

"Maybe I'll come to Puerto Rico and watch you play," Robert had suggested as he sauntered away.

"Cool!" Ashlee had nodded. Maybe, maybe not. He wasn't going to turn into

Mr Reliable overnight. But he was super-proud of her, she knew.

Ashlee had watched his back view as he walked to his car and engaged in heated conversation with the uniformed car-parking guy who was about to give him a ticket.

"So, you think you have a great future in basketball?" Theresa asked now in a low voice. She stared past Ashlee through the tiny window at the night sky. "Y'know, I found out on the school website that Queensbridge has a great high-school basketball team."

"It sure does," Ashlee grinned. Wow, was her mom on a steep learning curve! "If I get a place, I'll be able to study *and* play!"

"When," Theresa insisted. *"When* you get in!"

Ashlee nodded happily. "Fingers crossed. And I want to get even better," she confided. "To be as good as Michael Jordan. That's my true goal."

"To be the best?"

"To be as good as it's possible for me to be." To train her body, to refine her jumps and turns. To perfect all that. She would give it her best shot.

Ashlee felt the plane lose altitude, saw the nearside wing tilt away at a steep angle. Down below, the tiny orange lights of the city glittered. "So Mom, why don't you hit me with the guilt trip about me lying to you right now and get it over with?"

Theresa smiled faintly. "Let's skip it, shall we?"

Ashlee stared back. "Really?"

The wing flaps went down and the engines screamed.

"I'm a reformed character," Theresa insisted. "In future, I'll be so laid-back you won't know me."

The plane wheels hit the runway with a thump.

"Wow!" Ashlee muttered. "So tomorrow night I can go and train with the Saints without getting into a fight?"

Her mom nodded, then added one condition. "After you finish your homework."

"But I already sat the scholarship exam, remember?" They were on familiar territory as the plane taxied towards its gate.

"And we don't get the result through until next month," Theresa pointed out. "So we don't know yet whether you got the place at Queensbridge. Meanwhile, I don't want you to fall behind at the school you're in."

"Jeez, what happened to the new, laid-back you?" Ashlee groaned, reaching up to the overhead locker for her mom's bag.

A woman passenger across the aisle asked Ashlee for help. "Luckily you're tall enough to reach," she said with a smile.

Theresa leaned across. "My daughter's been selected to go to trials for the National Youth Basketball team!"

"Cool. Good luck to you!" The woman beamed back.

And Ashlee and her mom filed off the plane into the cold New York air. They were the same on the outside maybe, but inside, totally different.

"Goodnight," a member of the cabin crew said to each passenger as they stepped outside.

"Bye," Ashlee said. She went down the steps and onto the tarmac. The freezing wind blew hard, but her heart still soared and she felt as if she was walking on air.

Want to read more exciting sports stories?
Here's the first chapter from Donna King's
Kick Off!

Hey Lacey,
How are you doing, babe? How's Tampa Bay
without me? How's the beach? And have you
been down the mall today? Did you check out
the guys like we usually do – or like we usually
***did**, should I say?*

Tyra Fraser tapped away at the keyboard
furiously. In her head she could picture sun
and blue sea. Outside her window she saw
wet grey clouds, grey slate roofs and a
muddy grey river.

Oh gosh, you don't know how much I miss
Florida, she wrote. *England is the pits.*
Specifically Yorkshire – specifically Fernbridge!
How come you get to have a dad who runs a

pizza place in the best shopping mall in the entire world, and I have an army sergeant father who gets posted over here? How dumb is that?

I mean, it's September, for God's sakes, and it's freezing!!!!

Tomorrow I go to my new school. I am seriously gonna hate it, for sure.

Write me a long email, Lacey. Give me your news or I'll go crazy.

From your totally, hundred-and-ten percent miserable friend,

Tyra!!!! xxxx

"Tyra, honey, could you come down?"

Tyra trailed downstairs to the tiny kitchen in the poky house they now called home.

"I need to iron your dad's shirts. Can you watch Shirelle?"

"I'll take her for a walk," Tyra decided. Looking after her five-year-old, hyperactive kid sister in a space the size of a closet was asking for trouble. "C'mon, Shirry, let's go!"

No sooner said than the two girls were

out on the main street, heading for the park. They walked hand in hand past the butcher's shop and the grocery store, down the hill and over the old stone bridge. Shirelle pulled at Tyra's arm to stop her so they could stand and stare at the flotilla of ducks swimming under the arch. She wanted to dash across the road to see them come out the other side, but Tyra held her back – luckily, because just then, a guy on a motorbike whizzed past.

This is some hick town! Tyra thought. *One road through. One bus stop. One play area with swings and a rickety climbing-frame.* A few kids messed around in the park, kicking a ball and yelling.

"Push me!" Shirelle demanded, plonking herself on the nearest swing. "I wanna fly! Push harder!"

"Hold tight," Tyra warned. She felt spots of cold rain on her face and looked up at the steep hill that rose almost sheer out of the narrow valley. A thick mist rolled towards them.

"Cool!" Shirelle squealed, her pink day-glo sweater standing out against her light brown skin. Shirelle was the most colourful thing around, forming a bright downward arc in the dull air. She was into wild movement – running, leaping, splashing, yelling. She wasn't into sitting still, and boy, was she going to be a handful in her new junior school. Tyra was glad she wouldn't be there to see it. Instead, she'd be at the high school just down the road, along with a dozen other US Army kids whose parents worked at the early-warning base out on the Yorkshire moors.

"Watch out!" a voice called.

She turned from the swings in time to see a ball flying towards her. It looked as if it was going to be a direct hit on Shirelle, but at the last second Tyra jumped up and headed it to one side. The ball bounced harmlessly away.

A boy came running to fetch it. "Neat,"

he said with a surprised grin. "That was a cool header."

"Yeah, thanks."

Quickly the kid gathered his ball and ran off.

For a while, Tyra watched them play. *Now, soccer!* she thought, remembering once more the Astroturf with the Florida sun beating down, Lacey in midfield neatly passing her the ball, so she could forge ahead past defenders and blast the ball past the goalkeeper into the net. *Soccer is the one good thing about England! After all, it's the home of the greatest game in the world!*

"Higher!" Shirelle demanded, pushing with her feet and kicking her legs. "Tyra, make me fly!"

Hey girl! Lacey emailed back later that evening. *This does not sound like the Tyra I know! What's with the misery, dude? Where's the go-getting, world-beating kid that I remember?*

Seriously though, is it really bad?

Okay, so the weather's not exactly wall-to-wall sunshine over there, but they have cool music, don't they? And you get to watch English League soccer – Chelsea, Manchester United, Liverpool!

Yesterday I played as striker for the Tampa Bay Butterflies – your old position. We won three – zero. I scored two of the goals. I know that sounds like we're not missing you, but we are – big style! The girls said to say hi!

Okay, gotta go now, Tyra. Lots of luck tomorrow at the new school. Go, girl!

Love you – Lacey x x x

Walking into a place for the first time was always hard, Tyra told herself. The big glass entrance was buzzing with kids in uniform, which was the weirdest thing. At her high school in Florida, everyone had been able to wear whatever they liked. Here, the boys wore dark green blazers and grey pants – *trousers*, Tyra thought, correcting herself.

The girls wore white shirts and ties, with the same blazers as the boys. But they did the fashion thing with their skirts, wearing them short or long, narrow or wide, with their ties knotted loosely to show the top shirt-button. Self-consciously, Tyra fiddled to loosen her own tie.

The corridor ahead was wide and crowded.

"Walk, don't run!" the teachers shouted. But the kids ignored them. They slung their bags into their lockers, staring at Tyra and, by the scornful looks on their faces, giving her seriously low marks out of ten.

What's up? Do I have two heads? She glared back at a fair-haired girl who was giving her the evil eye.

"Are you the new girl?" the kid asked, looking like she was sucking lemons. "It's time for registration. Miss Jenkins said to fetch you."

Tyra nodded. Her long hair swung forward as she stooped to dump her bag in a low locker. "Hey, I'm Tyra," she announced as she stood up straight. "I'm from Tampa, Florida."

The girl stared.

What did I say – that I came from Mars? Tyra wondered, already crushed.

It got worse as she was led into the classroom. Here thirty heads turned. Thirty faces stared. Thirty classmates seemingly wrote her off.

"There's an empty desk here at the front," the teacher told her without looking up. "Thank you for that, Alicia. Please be sure to show Tyra around for the rest of the day."

At the back of the room, Alicia leaned over from her desk and muttered darkly to her friends. At the front, Tyra swallowed hard and tried not to notice.

"Mikey Swales has got the hots for you, Alicia!"

"No way!"

"He does. He told me!"

"When?"

"At morning break. He said for me to tell you."

Tyra stood to one side of the group of girls who were giggling in the playground. She shivered in the cold wind. Already she'd been told to tie her hair back by the deputy head teacher and yelled at for not paying attention during maths. The day was turning out even worse than she'd imagined.

"Anyway, Emma, you can tell Mikey I'm not interested," Alicia scoffed. "I wouldn't be seen dead with a weedy little geek like him."

Tyra winced. *Poor Mikey!*

"He's not a geek," a girl called Molly protested. She was tall, like Alicia, and seemed more likely to stand up to her than Emma, who was Little Miss Mouse. "He plays in the boys' football team for a start."

"Well, Molly, *you* go out with him then," Alicia shot back, making a beeline for one of the teachers on duty.

"It's not me he's got the hots for!" Molly laughed, dragging Tyra along with the crowd.

"Hey, sir!" Alicia yelled.

The teacher took no notice, but walked on with his green fleece jacket zipped up to his chin, cradling a mug of coffee between both hands.

Alicia went after him. "Mr Grey, we want to talk to you about the Under-13s girls' soccer team!"

Soccer! Tyra pricked up her ears.

With a pained expression the sports teacher turned. "Ah yes, the Under-13 girls. The magnificent eleven who were the Under-12s last year and managed not a single victory during the whole of last season!"

"That's because you concentrated too much on the boys!" Alicia reminded him. "You never gave us any proper coaching."

Mr Grey was obviously way past his sell-by date, Tyra decided. And he looked it, with his grey hair draped over his head to disguise his big bald patch, and his eye bags, and his belly hanging over his belt.

"Ah, the boys who won the English

Schools Football Association Coca-Cola Cup!" he reminded Alicia. "That was the remarkably talented team I wasted so much time on last year!"

"Ha-ha, very funny, sir!" Alicia frowned. "Anyway, this year we want proper coaching. Molly wants to go in goal and Emma wants to be midfield defence. I'm a centre forward – the main goal scorer!"

Yeah, why am I not surprised? Tyra thought. Alicia Webb had already gotten under her skin, and it was only Day One. Back home in Florida, Tyra had been top goal scorer of the Tampa Bay Butterflies.

Mr Grey sipped his coffee and shook his head. "I don't have anyone in the department who's interested in coaching you girls, I'm afraid."

"But that's not fair," Molly pointed out. "My mum says it's discrimination and it's not allowed!"

Right on! Tyra thought.

"Whoa!" The teacher took a step back.

"Quite the little feminist, aren't we, Molly Thomas?" His eye fell on a fellow member of staff patrolling the playground. He gave a cynical chuckle. "Then again, it doesn't have to be a member of the sports staff, does it? It could be, for instance, an *English* specialist!"

While Alicia shrugged at Molly and Emma, Mr Grey turned and beckoned to the passing teacher.

"Mr Wheeler, just the man for the job!" he announced. "I know you're new to Fernbridge and you haven't got properly settled yet, but I hear on the grapevine that you're the proud possessor of a Football Association Coaching Diploma!"

Blushing, the young teacher nodded. "Soccer's my thing," he acknowledged.

"He's young!" Alicia muttered.

"And cute!" Emma pointed out.

"Shut up and listen!" Molly told them.

Mr Grey seized his chance. "Luck is on your side, girls! Mr Wheeler here is a soccer coach. I'm sure he'd be willing to take on the Under-13 girls!"

"Erm . . . er . . . I would?" The chosen candidate seemed unsure.

"You would!" Mr Grey insisted. "So, Mr Wheeler, meet Alicia Webb, Molly Thomas and Emma Dean, who will be key players in your new team." He turned to Tyra with a vague look. "And you are . . . ?"

"Tyra Fraser," she stammered.

The shy new teacher smiled at the shy new pupil.

"Ignore her. She's from America. She doesn't play soccer," Alicia broke in as Mr Grey walked off.

She does, actually! Tyra protested silently. *And she's good, if you only cared to ask!*

The English teacher looked down at Alicia. "Actually, I hear they play a lot of soccer in US schools," he said.

Tyra nodded, but still couldn't speak. No, this was not a good start to her new school career.

"Oh, and good luck, Mr Wheeler," Mr Grey called from a distance. "Believe me, with the Under-13 girls, you're going to need it!"